GIDEON'S WRATH

Also by J. J. Marric

GIDEON'S DAY
GIDEON'S NIGHT
GIDEON'S WEEK
GIDEON'S MONTH
GIDEON'S RISK
GIDEON'S MARCH
GIDEON'S VOTE
GIDEON'S LOT
GIDEON'S STAFF

J. J. Marric

GIDEON'S WRATH

STEIN AND DAY/*Publishers*/New York

FIRST STEIN AND DAY PAPERBACK EDITION JUNE 1986

Gideon's Wrath is published by arrangement with
Harold Ober Associates.
Copyright © 1967 by John Creasey
All rights reserved.
Printed in the United States of America

Stein and Day, Incorporated
Scarborough House
Briarcliff Manor, N.Y. 10510

ISBN 0-8128-8267-9

ACKNOWLEDGMENTS

The author is extremely grateful to all those who advised him on the facts of this book, particularly the Friends of St. Paul's Cathedral, the vergers there and elsewhere, and the clergy and others at Westminster Abbey, Westminster Cathedral and the London Synagogue.

CHAPTER 1
THE WORSHIPER

The great nave was hushed and still. A pale light, tinted a dozen colors as it filtered through the ancient stained glass of the window, touched the stone wall and the threadbare standard of a long-vanished regiment once carried by a man of valor. The light, subtle as the harmony of an old tapestry, changed in depth where it fell upon the polished brass of a plate, which covered the last resting place of a politician who had done all that any politician could do to make himself right with God. Beyond this, the light faded into a dim, pale glow and vanished at the entrance to the private chapel of a saint seldom remembered.

This chapel was bare and bleak, empty save for a few dozen hard and shiny wooden chairs, a dark oak bench running round the walls like that in a court of law, and two or three paintings, each of the same saintly figure of half-forgotten history. The altar was covered with a cloth of handmade lace, and on it stood four candlesticks and a silver crucifix.

In front of the altar, at the rail, knelt a man.

There was so little light here that only those who came close could have noticed him. He knelt, in an awkward pose, on a tapestry hassock. One knee dented the middle of the hassock, the other edged to the cold stone floor. The man's hands were clasped on the rail, not in an attitude of prayer, but tightly, as if in physical pain or mental anguish.

His breathing was labored, almost sibilant. He had been in that position for a long time, as if unaware of the discomfort, his eyes sometimes closed and sometimes wide open. Now and again his lips moved.

"Oh, God," he would whisper; and after a long pause, "Oh, Christ."

After a longer pause, he would say, "What can I do? What the hell can I do?"

Suddenly, after a longer pause, his breathing became stertorous and he began to choke and groan, until words burst out of him.

"I've killed her!"

7

The sounds died away, as if the anguish had suffocated him. Then he whispered again: a name.

"Margaret . . . Oh, Margaret."

And then, hardly audible, "Oh, Christ, I've killed her."

His hands, still tightly clasped, slid off the polished altar rail and dropped to his raised knee. Save for his breathing he was silent, his eyes tightly closed as if to shut out even the darkness. Outside in the nave the pale colors glowed, and the hush was complete—until a footstep disturbed it rudely.

The man at the altar rail jerked his head up and turned. Another footfall sounded, and he moistened his lips.

A third footfall came and suddenly the filtering light was blotted out by darkness. The figure of a man showed black. The supplicant who had killed a woman now stared, teeth gritted in fear. A second later the light returned as the solitary man passed on, his footsteps hardly audible.

A verger?

A steward?

A priest?

Another worshiper?

Another sinner?

The man by the altar began to move, with great caution, helping himself by pulling against the rail. His knees, one warm, one cold, were stiff, his movements slow and clumsy. He listened intently for the slightest sound, heard none except the agitated beating of his own heart. The spell of anguish and remorse was broken, fear replacing it—dread that he might be seen or recognized; dread that retribution would soon catch up.

He crept to the door of the chapel, careful to avoid those beautiful colors; staring toward the choir and the high altar beyond. He heard nothing and for a while saw nothing, until suddenly a yellowish glow appeared, startling in the darkness, wavering as if held in an unsteady hand. Soon it settled on something which glistened, silent and golden. After a moment or two, shadows appeared; the glistening object moved, but not the light. Mesmerized by what was going on in front of him, the man by the chapel became aware of other things that glistened or glowed, all farther away from the radius of the pale light.

Another object disappeared; a rustling was followed by a faint clink of sound, a pause, a shadowy movement, another clink. Only after this had happened several times did the man who had killed realize what was happening; it was as if a voice within him cried:

He's stealing the altar plate!

The fact, to him, was so monstrous that the enormity of his own crime was momentarily forgotten. Here, under his very eyes, was sacrilege. His mouth opened; a cry rose within him but, gripped by an instinct that valued his personal safety above everything else on earth, he did nothing. The light moved, and so keen was his sense of perception and so much better his vision that he could make out the hands and fingers, even the shape of the thief's head and shoulders as the area of his depredations widened.

The man who had taken life turned his back on the man who was robbing the cathedral. He crept toward the door that was left open by the crypt so that those in spiritual need could come by night for solace or for help. Only when he reached the narrow wooden door, carved by a monk five centuries before, did he turn round. A strange and awe-inspiring sight met his gaze. There was more light. It came from the moon, risen higher in the heavens. This moonlight shone through the stained glass of a dozen windows and cast a lovely pattern on the floor, the walls, the great pillars, the brass, the memorial wording cut deep into the walls. The thief by the altar, quite oblivious, was shifting his torch so that he could see still farther afield.

The murderer by the door pushed it, and the hinges creaked faintly. He caught his breath, but the man inside did not pause. Cautiously the murderer pushed open the outer, much heavier, door and stepped into London's night.

It was cold. He shivered. He turned toward the main steps and the main doors, the shivering worsening like ague. His teeth chattered. His hands felt icy. In the distance, a car engine sounded and soon a car hummed by, its headlights dipped and dim against the light from tall street lamps. The red light disappeared, and the man by the cathedral steps looked toward the emptiness of Ludden Hill and Ludden Circus.

Across the road, the light of a telephone kiosk shone, hard and warning. He crossed to it, fingering the coins in his pocket, hesitated, then pulled open the narrow door. More light sprang up so that he could see the notices, how to dial, how to put money in the slots, how to call the police.

Dial 999. Of course.

He lifted the receiver, hand steadier now, and put the tip of his forefinger in the hole. 9—brrrk. 9—brrrk. 9—brrrk.

Almost on the instant, a man said briskly, "Scotland Yard."

"I want—I want to report a burglary," the man said in a hoarse agitated voice.

"Thank you, sir. If you will give your name—"

"At St. Ludd's!" the man cried. "There's a thief in St. Ludd's!"

He thrust the receiver down with frenzied vigor as the disembodied voice asked him for his name. For a dreadful instant he had nearly answered, so deeply ingrained was habit. He had nearly said, "This is Eric Greenwood." It did not then occur to him how unlikely it was that they would associate him with Margaret's lifeless body, her swollen throat. He swung round, pushing the door open, stepping out. A policeman stood only twenty yards in front of him, advancing slowly from the faint white stone of a great new group of buildings.

For a split second, the murderer stood rigid. The policeman, without quickening his pace, drew nearer. The murderer, nervous tension near to screaming point, turned suddenly on his heel and went back the way he had come, the voice inside him warning:

"Don't hurry. Don't panic." All the time, his heart beat time to the refrain, racing so wildly that the self-injunctions ran into one another. *Don't hurry—don't panic—don't run. Don't hurry don't panic don't run. Don't run don't run. Runrunrunrunrun.* Because he knew the district well, he turned right, toward the Mansion House, passing the new buildings there; only when he was on the other side of the road did he look round.

The policeman had not followed him.

He turned again, and heard a car approaching at great speed, from Ludden Circus. He also heard a squeal of tires, and glanced over his shoulder to see a car pulling up in front of St. Ludd's. The police, he thought, the police he had summoned, they would catch the thief who had dared to commit sacrilege but not the man who had disobeyed the command, *Thou shalt not kill.* As he made his way, something of the earlier anguish and fear and remorse returned, but the anguish was not so acute, not so obsessive. He could think, as well as feel. He could recall the picture of Margaret's face, so round and pretty and so gay, and the sudden change in it to distress, as she had said, "I can't go on, Eric, my darling! I can't go on."

It had been like a great iron ball, smashing into his head.

"You must understand," she had pleaded. "I can't go on deceiving Geoffrey like this. I can't look him in the face. It was bad enough when he was away, but now he's home again it's impossible."

He had thought in a spasm of wild fury, "She wants to leave me. She wants *him!*"

"You're tired of me! That's the truth, you're tired of me!"

"No. It isn't that. It's just that I can't go on cheating him—
and I *can't* leave the children. Eric, you know I can't. Eric.
Eric!" Suddenly, as his hands had closed about her throat, her
voice had risen to a scream. *"Eric!"*

Now, she lay dead.

Now, he had prayed.

Now, he had to save himself from the consequences of his
wickedness.

Although London slept and the great churches were as
empty as the great blocks of offices, the museums, the stores
and schools, the halls and stately homes, at one place there
was an ever-watchful eye. That was Scotland Yard, the headquarters of the Metropolitan Police. In fact, however, only
one section of the building was wide awake: the section which
housed the Information Room and the offices of the Criminal
Investigation Department. From here, the center of the web
of London's police, the Divisions and the subdivisional police
stations were controlled. Each constable on duty in uniform
or in plain clothes, each sergeant and officer of higher rank,
was directed from one of these police stations, which themselves were directed from Scotland Yard.

A police constable named Glenn, on duty that night at St.
Ludd's, was in fact from the City of London Police, another
force; but the three men who appeared in the powerful car,
just after he had seen the man come from the telephone
kiosk, were from the Yard. The two forces worked very
closely together, sometimes almost as if they were one. The
first car had only just stopped when another, from the City,
pulled up on the other side of St. Ludd's, close to the Crypt
Gate. At once, the men began to station themselves by the
exits, and Glenn joined a man who stood by the statue of
Queen Anne.

"What's up?"

"Had a tip-off."

"What about?"

"Burglar in there." "There" was indicated by a jerk of the
thumb.

"Blimey!"

"If it's not a hoax," the other remarked. "You seen
anyone?"

"Saw a chap come out of the kiosk. He was in a hell of a
hurry."

"Probably the one who tipped us off," the Yard man remarked. "Get a good look at him?"

"Not bad."

"Might come in useful."

Still another car arrived and two big men got out, going up the steps immediately and conferring with a man already by the main entrance to the cathedral. The whispering of voices sounded clear on the still air, and the shapes of the men were sharply defined in the soft light of the moon. Out of the gloom at one side of the cathedral a man in a dressing gown appeared, tousled, bright-eyed. He was a verger disturbed by a call from the police. The whispering continued.

"What doors are open?"

"Only one, on the south side. Near the High Altar."

"Quite sure of that?"

"Well, it's the only door that *should* be open."

"We'll put a man at each of the others and try the one on the south side," decided Detective Inspector Goodways of the City Police. "No need for you yet, sir. We'll use torches, be easier to surprise this chap. If you'd care to put some clothes on—"

"But I can't believe—"

"Have to make sure, sir," Goodways insisted.

"Yes, of course," the verger said. "Very well, I'll get dressed and send for the canon." He turned away again, obviously reluctant to admit that there might be a thief, as obviously determined not to be obstructive. As he disappeared a whispered order was sent out, and soon four men converged on the door through which the murderer had escaped. Detective Inspector Goodways and Detective Sergeant Hodgson from the Metropolitan Force went in, making very little sound for such big and heavy men. But as they stepped into the cathedral itself, someone brushed the door and it clanged sharply.

A yellow light, some distance off, seemed to glow brightly; then it went out.

"He's heard us," Goodways whispered. "Go ahead."

On that instant, first he and then Hodgson switched on powerful torches as Hodgson called in a deep, carrying voice which echoed with strange resonance: "Don't move! We know you're there."

One torch beam shone on a pale statue, the other on the figure of a man carrying a big suitcase. At first, he did not move; it was as if he realized that he had no choice but to give himself up. However, as the two detectives went toward him, and two more of lesser rank followed them in, the thief uttered an obscenity in a shrill, scared voice.

"——you!"

He turned and began to run toward the great doors of St. Ludd's. The hurried, uncoordinated sound fell as desecration in that house of prayer.

CHAPTER 2
GIDEON

No one with the name of Gideon could be oblivious of the fact that to many people the Biblical connotation sprang immediately to mind. There were even those who said that, given a flowing beard, a voluminous gown and a thick and heavy staff, the Gideon who was a Commander at Scotland Yard would make a passable Old Testament prophet. Hearing this Gideon would laugh, but it never failed to touch him with uneasiness. He was of an age, in his early fifties, and of a nonconformist religious upbringing, which could give a puritanical slant to most matters having to do with religion, and he hoped he was neither as puritanical nor as forbidding as many of the Old Testament prophets seemed to him.

It was characteristic of the man, physically so massive and powerful, mentally absolutely sure of himself in his job, that he should be sufficiently introspective to wonder whether any aspect of his character influenced the way he did that job.

On the morning after the attempted theft of the altar plate from the Cathedral and the murder of Mrs. Margaret Entwhistle, nothing was farther from Gideon's mind. He had a family preoccupation as well as an administrative one, and it was the first of these that occupied his mind at the moment. He wanted to concentrate on a matter of high policy in the Criminal Investigation Department but was unable to forget the face of his youngest daughter.

Poor, sad Penny; she had just failed her Royal College examination in music, an examination which was to have set her on the road to a career as a professional pianist. The letter with the results of the examination had arrived just before Gideon left home, and so he had been delayed, which was exasperating in itself. He remembered the sight of Penelope's glowing blue eyes, so like her mother's, the radiance of her face as she had opened the letter. Gideon and Kate, his wife, less sure than their daughter of the result, had watched her.

She had read. . . .

Her face had dropped; her expression had become one almost of despair. She hadn't trusted herself to look up at her parents, just stared at the letter.

"No luck, Penny?" Gideon had asked gruffly.

"No."

"Oh, what a shame!" Kate had cried. "They can't have——"

"I must have been really bad. And it was easy. I only had to play a selection from Liszt's *Hungarian Rhapsodies. . . .*" Penelope broke off.

"Better luck next time," Gideon had said, bleakly aware of the inadequacy of his words.

"There won't be a next time," Penelope had said, drearily. "I've failed, and that's that. Malcolm always said I was ham-handed on the piano, and this has proved it. I'll just have to give up. It doesn't matter really."

Suddenly she had darted away from the front room of the Harrington Street house, run up the stairs and into her room. Creaking springs told that she had flung herself on her bed. Husband and wife had looked at each other, unhappily, and then Kate had forced herself to speak.

"She'll be all right, George."

"Yes, I suppose so."

"She always was too sure of herself. This might do her good."

"I'd like five minutes with those examiners," Gideon had growled, and then suddenly laughed at himself. "I must go! Call me at the office if you think I can help."

"I'll look after her, dear."

And Kate would; no one better.

Gideon reflected on this as he parked his car near the main entrance of the old Commissioner's Office Building, soon to be demolished, or at least vacated by the police for stark new premises farther along the river. He must get the girl out of his mind. The funny thing was that when one's own child was hurt, one was so deeply, unreasonably affected, even when that child was an adult. Penelope was twenty-one—a young woman, not an infant to fuss over and protect.

The courtyard was crowded with big men, standing by or moving to and from cars, two of which were being dusted. The police sergeant on duty said "Good morning," and Gideon nodded. The morning was bright and the sky a vivid blue, but for him the dull red brick of the buildings cast a gloom. He walked up the tall flight of steps, noting that the hands of the clock in the hall touched nine-thirty—later than he had intended. Four Jamaicans, spruce and very well-dressed, their dark faces showing an almost polished brightness, were sitting round the big table, talking earnestly; they were West Indian delegates here for a police conference. A constable said:

"Good morning, sir."

"Morning."

Gideon's office was up one floor, overlooking the Embankment and the Thames, just now shimmering with sunlight and gay with pleasure boats. Gideon hardly gave the view a glance as he sat at his desk of polished mahogany, seeing a pile of reports and documents in front of his chair. On the top was a note in heavy black lettering: 10 A.M. COMMISSIONER'S OFFICE.

So he wasn't to have much breathing space before plunging into the administrative problem.

He pulled his chair up and paused to reflect, putting one hand on the report pile. There were at least a dozen different cases here, each requiring his immediate attention. Half would need studying closely, and he would probably have to talk to the Superintendent-in-Charge of at least six investigations. Allow half an hour for each of these cases, and that would see the morning out. Allow an hour with the Commissioner, and he wouldn't get round to the last case until mid-afternoon. He glanced up, forgetting that he now had a room of his own, that his assistant had been moved next door. He pressed the bell-push as he lifted a telephone. The door leading from his assistant's room opened instantly, the operator answering at the same time.

"Get me the Commissioner's office." Gideon raised a hand to the tall, lanky man who came in, bony-faced, bright-eyed, thinning black hair smoothed down with too much hair cream, red and white spotted bow tie a little too flamboyant. This was Chief-Superintendent Lemaitre. "Sit," said Gideon, and a moment later, "Colonel Scott-Marle, please . . . Gideon." Lemaitre sat down and Gideon asked, "Who's waiting to see me?"

"Rollo, Simmons and Golightly," answered Chief-Superintendent Lemaitre. "As you were late I dealt with the others."

Gideon nodded.

"Yes, Gideon," said Colonel Sir Reginald Scott-Marle in his rather aloof voice; over the telephone most people found him hard to approach.

"Is ten o'clock the only possible time, sir?" Gideon asked.

"Isn't it convenient for you?"

"I can make it convenient, but there are one or two urgent jobs I'd rather attend to first."

"Then make it eleven," Scott-Marle said. "And let me know what the Dean says."

He rang off before there was time to answer. Gideon frowned as he replaced the receiver. Lemaitre was looking at him, eyebrows raised, lips parted in a set smile. What had the Commissioner meant by "Let me know what the Dean says"? He did not ask Lemaitre if he knew; one way to preserve an oracle-like reputation was to find out the difficult answers for oneself.

"What's Golightly want?" he inquired.

"He's been over to M1 Division. A woman was strangled there last night," said Lemaitre. "Looks as if the husband did it."

Gideon made no comment except a mental one: that remark, prejudging an issue about which he could not possibly have enough evidence, was characteristic of Lemaitre. It also made it easier for Gideon to form a decision when he saw Scott-Marle. He wondered if Lemaitre realized what the morning's conference was about. The Yard was a spawning ground for rumor, and none spawned so prodigally as those about appointments in the Force.

"I'll see Golightly first," decided Gideon. "Get him for me."

"Right." Lemaitre went smartly to the door. "We can't keep the Commissioner waiting too long, can we?"

Was there a slightly malicious, or hurt, expression in his voice and in his eyes?

Gideon half wondered as he picked up the first file, marked: *Murder : Margaret Entwhistle. C. Supt. Golightly,* the second, marked: *Murder—Photo-Nudes: C. Supt. Rollo,* and the third, marked: *Fraud: C. Supt. Simmons.* The file beneath this was one he hadn't seen before, marked: *Attempted theft: St. Ludd's Cathedral.* He needed no more telling what Scott-Marle had meant about the Dean; obviously the Commissioner had assumed he would need time to start on this particular investigation. Yet another swift thought, more a reaction, passed through Gideon's mind: this kind of crime was sacrilege, about which the public conscience was likely to be very sensitive. The case would need careful handling.

The door opened, and Golightly came in.

It had often seemed to Gideon that names either fitted perfectly or were complete misfits. Golightly's fitted like a glove. He was a comparatively small man by the standard of physique in the C.I.D.; neat, bland, gentle, soft-voiced; one seldom heard him approaching, so quiet were his movements. He was in his late forties, fair-haired, with innocent-looking

gray eyes which always seemed to have a hint of surprise in
them.

"Morning, Percy."

"Morning, Commander."

Gideon was looking through the thin file.

"Sit down."

"Thanks."

A married woman, attractive according to the photograph,
had been found in her bed, strangled. Her husband, darkly
handsome judging from a snapshot of him, said he had come
in at three o'clock in the morning and found her dead in bed.
Their three children, aged eleven, six, and three, had been
sound asleep—two girls in one room and the boy, the eleven-
year-old, in his own. The husband, Geoffrey Entwhistle, had
telephoned the police. The Divisonal murder squad had gone
over at once—arriving at three-thirty-one precisely.

"No one lost much time," Gideon remarked. "When did
you get there?"

"Just after seven."

"Couldn't you sleep?"

Golightly smiled dutifully.

"I'm still an early riser, and I called Information in case I
could do anything on the way here. So I looked in at Entwhistle's place."

Gideon's eyes were smiling.

"Just to pass the time of morning."

"You know how the Divisions like someone to hold their
hand," rejoined Golightly. "I haven't a big job on at the moment, you know."

That was true. Moreover, this was his kind of job: the family crime, an investigation which affected people suffering
from too much emotion. Such a condition was very relevant
in Percy Golightly's opinion; he was hypersensitive to the undertones prevalent in crimes of passion, and in a way he enjoyed burrowing into the causes of such crimes, perhaps because each taught him a little more about human beings and
so helped him in his job.

"Think this one's right for you?" asked Gideon.

"It could be."

"Lem thinks the husband's worth keeping an eye on."

"So do I," said Golightly. "And the lover boy."

"What?" ejaculated Lemaitre, from the door.

"So there's another man involved," Gideon remarked.

"Not much doubt about it from what the neighbors say,"
Golightly told him.

"There's the motive, then!" exclaimed Lemaitre.

"The lover's or the husband's?" asked Golightly, with his mildly perplexed and faintly knowing smile. "M1 is deep in that bank robbery, Commander, that Division's got enough on its plate. This job isn't really right for them, anyway. They can give me all the help I'll need, but Fisherton would be glad to leave it to me."

"I dare say," said Gideon dryly. Fisherton, the Superintendent at M1 Division, was nearing retirement, and since having a serious operation two years before, had lost much of his vigor. He never missed a chance of passing the buck on any job. Golightly, cunning as he was, had anticipated the likely result of his call—probably Fisherton had telephoned Golightly at home. Gideon had to decide quickly whether to let him and Fisherton have their way, or make the Division take the responsibility. The real question was whether Golightly would do the better job; there was no point in being stubborn or cussed.

Gideon reached his decision.

"You take over," he said. "Get any help necessary from the Division; if you need any from here I want to know in advance."

Golightly smiled much more freely.

"Thanks a lot," he said, and stood up.

Lemaitre watched him go, leaned back in his chair, exploded: "Lover boy!" and jumped up. "I'll go get Rollo."

Rollo was one of the Yard's glamour boys, the most worldly and probably the most licentious member of the C.I.D. His reputation as a bachelor made even hardened policemen whistle, shocking some and making others envious, but he had a professional etiquette as rigid as any doctor's. His *affaires de coeur*, as he referred to them, were strictly out of business hours; he was as cold-blooded with a beautiful woman witness as with a plain one. His peccadilloes affected his work in this, however: he *did* know women, particularly the sophisticated and those who were promiscuous by nature. The photo-nude murders probably concerned such women. Unlike the case which had preoccupied the Yard for years, that of the murder of prostitutes whose nude bodies were found in many parts of London, these were of young girls who were easily persuaded to be photographed in the nude. At least three had died soon after being photographed—of narcotic poisoning. The first two had been taken for suicides by overdoses of sleeping tablets; a third, in such identical circumstances, made murder much more likely. Chief Superintendent Hugh Rollo was now in charge of the case. He was a youthful-looking forty-five, pleasant-faced rather than handsome, with a deep, melodious voice.

"What's new?" Gideon asked him.

"I've found a professional photographer we knew nothing about who has a collection of nude photographs that would rock the Folies Bergère," answered Rollo. "He works part-time in the photographic department of a big chemist shop and has access to every poison in the pharmaceutical book. He's got a nice little picture gallery in a cellar at his home —still lives with his parents, though. I'd like to check if he's got any pictures of the three girls who died."

This was one way of asking for a search warrant, but there was probably more in the request than that.

"What else?" Gideon demanded.

Rollo laughed. "Call this a confession. One of his models used to be an acquaintance of mine. I don't know what you feel about my mixing past pleasures with business."

Gideon grinned. "Don't mix 'em too intimately," he said. "Does this chap know he's under suspicion?"

"I doubt it."

"Don't forget how badly we want the killer," Gideon said, and waved his hand in dismissal.

As Rollo stood up, two telephones on Gideon's desk rang. Gideon answered the exchange telephone, Lemaitre the internal one.

"Gideon."

"Commander's Office."

"Commander, the very Reverend the Dean of St. Ludd's is on the line."

"Hold him for one moment." Gideon picked up the other telephone. "Gideon."

"This is the Back Room, Commander. I've got a bunch of press reporters here screaming for a statement on the attempted theft at St. Ludd's."

"Tell 'em they can't have one for at least an hour," Gideon ordered. He rang off, placed one hand over the mouthpiece of the other instrument, and looked across at Lemaitre, who was holding his telephone and obviously waiting to get a word in. "What is it, Lem?"

"Simmons says he's onto something. Can he see you later, and not hang about for you now?"

"Yes."

"Okay, Simmy," Lemaitre said into his mouthpiece.

"Put the Dean through now, please," Gideon said.

He noticed that Big Ben was striking ten; it was a good thing he had postponed the discussion with Scott-Marle.

CHAPTER 3
DELICATE MISSION

"Good morning, Mr. Howcroft," Gideon said.

"Good morning, Mr. Gideon," said the Very Reverend Dean. "You have some idea why I am worrying you, no doubt."

"No worry at all, sir."

"That's most reassuring," the Dean murmured; his voice was slow, and slightly husky. "May I come and see you this morning?"

"How soon can you be here?"

"In five minutes or so, if that would suit you. I am at Westminster Abbey at this moment."

Gideon did not understand why he was so surprised, but surprised he was and it took him a moment or two to say, "I'll be free until five minutes to eleven, sir, when I have to leave for a conference."

"Most cooperative of you. I know how busy you must be. Shall I come to any particular entrance?"

"The Commissioner's entrance—the man on duty in the yard will direct you, and I'll have someone waiting in the hall to bring you straight up."

"Thank you again," Dean Howcroft said.

Gideon rang off, rubbed his chin, saw Lemaitre staring at him with more than customary intensity, and smothered a sigh. There were mornings which were simple routine, one could just get on with the job, but too many were like this. Penelope, the administration problem, the fresh murder, the Cathedral crime. He looked back at his assistant, friend, and confidant of many years, feeling almost as if he were about to betray him. It was a nonsensical thought, but he could not rid himself of it. The best thing now was to face the matter squarely.

"Well, Lem," he said. "Know what the meeting with Scott-Marle is about?"

"I can guess," Lemaitre answered, avoiding Gideon's eyes.

"And you'd be right. The decision about the new Deputy Commander can't be put off much longer."

"And it's not going to be me."

"No, it isn't," Gideon agreed. He hated himself, yet went on defensively, "We've talked this out a dozen times, and you've always agreed you don't want the job."

"That's right, *I'm* the liar," Lemaitre muttered.

He wanted the post desperately, of course, despite the fact that reason told him he was not right for it. He knew that well enough. Now and again, after an abysmal failure to handle a major investigation successfully, he would quip bluffly that he wasn't cut out for responsibility, that he was the natural assistant, born to subservience. Yet here was a dream of a lifetime, fading; after this morning, all hope, all illusion and all self-deception would be gone. The bony face seemed to become thinner, almost haggard, and the full lips worked.

"Lem," Gideon said gently, "I don't think the job is right for you."

"Too true you don't. Why not let me have it straight? You don't think I'm right for the job of Deputy Commander, in line for promotion to Commander. Let's have it, George, the blunt truth."

Gideon, so deeply concerned, studied his friend, and then said quietly, "I think Alec Hobbs is right for it."

"Dear old school tie."

Out of nowhere, Gideon felt a flash of annoyance not far removed from anger, and it must have shown in his expression, for suddenly Lemaitre jumped up, clapped his bony hands together, forced a broad grin, and said boisterously, "Old bloody school tie be damned! You and I went to the same type of school, George, London Elementary in the days before they knew what a grammar school was! Hobbs is the man for the job. I know it, and the fact that I'm *not* the man for it isn't your fault or Hobbs's. There's just one thing. Don't ask me to kowtow to the slob." Suddenly he looked forlorn and anxious; he broke off again.

Gideon said, "You kowtow to anyone? That'll be the day!"

Lemaitre drew a deep breath and stood very still. Then his whole body relaxed, and Gideon knew the crisis was past. He thought (without consciously thinking), "Thank God." He gave a little smile, stood up, and with a gesture rare in him, placed a hand on Lemaitre's shoulder.

"Do you know Dean Howcroft?" he inquired.

"I'd know his face in a church, if that's what you mean."

"He's probably in the front hall, now. Go and bring him up, will you?"

Lemaitre's eyes lost their strained unhappiness.

"Come to hallow the ground of the old place, has he? Must say he's taken his time. Okay, George." He strode to the door, hesitated, turned round and said in a voice in which amusement overlay a suddenly revealed truth, "Now there is a man I might kowtow to!" He went out and, before the door closed, began to whistle.

Gideon felt a marked lessening of tension.

He had two or three minutes in which to clear his mind of Lemaitre and the administration problem and to prepare for the Dean. Standing in front of the desk, he skimmed through the file, which simply reported the facts: an unknown man had telephoned at one-twenty-one, saying that a thief was inside St. Ludd's Cathedral. The caller had seemed breathless and agitated. The Flying Squad had been alerted, and cars from the City Police as well as from the Yard had converged on the Cathedral. Entry had been made from the south door, near the Lady Chapel, by a detective sergeant from West Central Division, and by Detective Inspector Goodways of the City of London Police; Gideon knew both men by sight. The thief, caught red-handed, had attempted to escape and had been cornered by a City policeman at the northwest door. He was an old lag with a record as long as his arm. Gideon glanced down the list of his offenses but saw none involving a church.

There was a sharp tap at the door.

"Come in!" he called.

"Here we are, sir," said Lemaitre, as if he hadn't a care in the world. "The Commander's expecting you." The door opened wide. "Commander Gideon, the Very Reverend Dean of St. Ludd's."

Gideon held out his hand.

Dean Howcroft, a man in his early sixties, would have stood out in any gathering simply because of his snowy white hair; quite beautiful hair which had a natural wave and was brushed straight back from his forehead, like a lion's mane. He was not, in other respects, particularly good-looking, for beneath an exceptionally broad forehead his nose was snub and his chin rather vague; nevertheless his appearance was that of a fine-looking man. He had a reputation for pungency in his comments on social behavior, a pungency which fell short of placing him among one of the lunatic fringe which lapped the church.

He was shorter than Gideon, and perhaps a little too well-fed, for both his collar and his clerical-gray jacket fitted over-closely. There was an unexpected briskness about his manner, however, and warmth in his smile.

"So we meet again, Mr. Gideon."

"The last time was at the wedding of the Home Secretary's

daughter," Gideon remarked, pleased that the other had remembered him. "Do sit down."

"Thank you. This is an unhappy business, I'm afraid."

Gideon said cautiously, "Any crimes attached to a church could be considered so."

"Yes, indeed. I understand you caught the man."

"We did."

"Such very quick work," approved the Dean.

"Thank you." Gideon was wondering what all this was leading up to. At the back of his mind there was Scott-Marle's reference to the Dean; someone had told the Commissioner in advance.

"Do you know the man?"

"He's an habitual criminal."

"Are you sure?" The Dean's voice sharpened and he looked taken aback.

"We certainly are." Gideon tapped the file. "Four times in jail; the last time he was sentenced he asked for seventeen other cases to be taken into account. He could hardly be more professional. He's always stolen silver or jewelry. I don't know him personally, but I shall soon have a report from someone who does. Have you any special interest in this man?"

"No," said the Dean. He frowned, and myriad wrinkles appeared at his eyes and forehead. "Only in what he did last night. I am interested in certain other offenses which may affect you, Commander. I have just been to the Abbey, as you know, where I discussed with the Dean a problem common to many of the big churches, perhaps more common than we like to admit. It is somewhat ironic that I've come to you as a consequence of a very different kind of offense, very different indeed."

Why not say "crime," wondered Gideon.

"Why have you come, sir?"

"On a somewhat delicate mission from our point of view, perhaps a very ordinary one to you. I asked Sir Reginald Scott-Marle whom I should see, and he unhesitatingly said that I should see you."

"Oh." That was one little mystery cleared. "What's the delicate problem, sir?"

"Commander," said the Dean, leaning forward and looking very earnest, "the Church—all churches—have many problems, perhaps the greatest being that of our relationship with the people. Forgive a blunt question, please. Are *you* a Christian?"

Gideon, momentarily taken aback, recovered and smiled at the directness of the approach.

"Nominally, yes, I suppose."

"Ah," said Dean Howcroft, repeating with a certain ironic inflection: "Nominally. One of the great host of nominal Christians." He hesitated, his slate-gray eyes searching, and the wrinkles puckered his forehead again. "And yet from my knowledge of you and your reputation, I would not have thought you would be nominal about anything."

"Can *I* be blunt, sir?"

"Please."

"I'm a policeman. I deal with criminals from all classes and all religions—Christians from all sects, Jews, Mohammedans, Buddhists, Hindus—I repeat, sir, *all* religions. Under the law, all men are equal whether they have any religion of none. As a policeman, I am committed to neutrality. That means nominal, surely."

After a long pause, Howcroft said, "And as a man?"

"I'm a policeman first, and you have come to see me as a policeman."

"No," said Howcroft, quite sharply. "That is evading the question." When Gideon stared at him expressionlessly, he went on: "I'm sorry, Commander, truly sorry—and of course I, too, am being evasive in my own way. It is perhaps a simpler question than I am making it out to be. The Church cannot be quite so ruthless in its attitudes as other organizations. We cannot come to the police with the same alacrity as could, say, a business house or a hotel. We have a wider, more embracing duty to all people, even when they break the law."

He paused, allowing a chance for interruption; Gideon let it go.

"And we have to worry about our public image, too. If we are severe with offenders, we are likely to be judged too harsh; if we try to help by understanding, we are judged too lenient. Either way, our image is smeared; and yet we need a clear, true image, Commander. Don't you agree?"

Gideon said, "I hope you do, sir."

"What do you mean by that?"

Gideon gave a grim little smile. "A true image isn't necessarily a good one, is it? In the moral sense."

After a moment's pause, the Dean smiled more freely than he had since entering the room.

"No indeed," he conceded. "But I will settle for an accurate one. I like to think you would find it good enough. I shouldn't have asked you if you were a Christian, you know, it was the wrong word. People are apt to jib at it." He went

on quickly: "But I mustn't waste your time. Commander, in
the past few months there have been a great number of
trifling—I say trifling in the material sense—acts of vandalism
in many churches. St. Paul's, the Abbey, Westminster Cathedral, St. Martin-in-the-Fields—all of these have suffered. So
have many parish churches, both Church of England and, I
believe, those of the Roman Catholic faith. Those of us who
have to minister to the material needs of the Church are increasingly disturbed by these acts. No single case is sufficient
to justify calling you in, but the sum total of damage and loss
is becoming quite considerable. We have tried and failed to
discover the culprits. We know we must now consult the
Yard. I have been tempted to do so several times. Last night's
sacrilege made it possible for me to see you, officially. I have
talked with my very good friends the Deans of the Abbey and
of St. Paul's. They agree that it would be wise to be wholly
frank with you. Do you think you can help us to find out who
is doing this—in fact to find out whether it is organized or
whether all the incidents are unconnected—and at the same
time help us to avoid notoriety and disfavor with our—ah—
nominal supporters?"

CHAPTER 4
RIGHT MAN?

Gideon studied the alert, eager face, sensing the depth of the
Dean's feeling, his anxiety to solve the problem and yet by so
doing to cause no adverse criticism; to do good, without any
risk of harm. That phrase entered Gideon's mind, and it
seemed to him that it epitomized the attitude and the thinking
of this rather prolix man. As he sat, considering, Howcroft
could not keep quiet.

"I have made myself clear, haven't I? You do understand,
don't you?"

"You've made yourself very clear, and I think I know
exactly what you want," Gideon said. Suddenly he smiled
broadly, appreciating the other's acumen. "And you've timed
it perfectly! We can now take a closer interest in St. Ludd's
and the other big churches, without arousing anyone's suspicions."

"Precisely! And will you?"

"Suits us best, too," Gideon pointed out. "We also have to worry about our image, and if we get the reputation of spending too much time going after sneak thieves in the churches instead of concentrating on the big criminals in business and society—"

He broke off, for the Dean was chuckling.

"Sir Reginald was right indeed," he said. "I'm most grateful. It goes without saying that I will do everything I can to help, and I can promise you the same from my ecclesiastic colleagues and friends. In our rather fumbling and amateur way we have already attempted—"

Gideon, an eye on the clock, interrupted. "First things first, sir. We need the right man to look after this, someone with sufficient general knowledge of church background, regalia and customs—" He was thinking aloud and at the same time considering senior officers who might be familiar with the set-up and have the right temperament for dealing with churchmen. "Give me a little while to think about it. We want someone who is sympathetic but whose emotions won't run away with him."

"Another nominal Christian, to be sure," the Dean said, his eyes twinkling.

Gideon chuckled, and had a rare feeling: that here was a man whom he could grow to like very much, one who had both humor and humility.

"Up to you to convert him from nominal to practicing," he said, and stood up. "If you'll let me have your telephone number and an address where I can always get you, I'll be in touch very soon."

The Very Reverend Dean of St. Ludd's took a fat envelope from a mysteriously hidden pocket and handed it across the desk.

"You will find everything you need in there, Commander, including the results of our own tentative investigations—futile, I assure you, hence our belated realization that professional help was needed." His handshake was firm, the twinkle remained. "I will find my own way out—"

"Mr. Lemaitre will show you the way," Gideon said, and opened Lemaitre's door. "Superintendent, you've met Dean Howcroft, haven't you?"

Lemaitre's big hand shot out, engulfing the Dean's. "Very glad to know you, sir. Not often an ex-choir boy has the chance to shake hands with the Dean. It was Dean Ruston in my day, sir. Lived to be about a hundred!"

"He did indeed," said Howcroft, marveling. "And you are an old choir boy at St. Ludd's? How very unexpected. You must come along and hear the choir again one day, we have two very beautiful voices—*very* beautiful indeed."

He went out with Lemaitre. Gideon stared at the closing passage door, remembering. Lemaitre had often mentioned the days when he had been a choir boy. Such a childhood experience lay in many a tough man's recollection, covered by cynical comment or crude joke. Lemaitre, ex-St. Ludd's, was certainly no more than a nominal Christian, but his wife—his second wife—was a regular churchgoer. Well, well.

Gideon laughed suddenly: he was thinking in much the same way as the Dean talked.

It was five to eleven—time he went along to see Scott-Marle.

At five to eleven Eric Greenwood stood up from his desk in a tiny office which overlooked the Thames and a corner of Billingsgate Market, and stepped into the even smaller office where his secretary sat at a typewriter which never seemed silent. Stubby fingers poised over the keys, she looked up. She was fifty-three, plump, coarse-skinned, gray-haired—and quite incredibly efficient. She had been secretary to the previous manager of this department, and by now was considered to be part of the furniture of Cox and Shielding, Importers and Exporters from the Orient. Behind her broad, innocently shining forehead there was more knowledge of out-of-the-way suppliers of exotic commodities than in any other brain in London.

"Yes, Mr. Greenwood?"

"I'm going across to see Shalimar's. Hold any calls, Bessie."

"Yes, Mr. Greenwood."

Before the flimsy door closed she was hammering away at the typewriter again, yet when her letters were finished they would be type-perfect. Greenwood stepped into a very narrow passage, with doors at regular intervals, each marked with the name of the department. There were Spices, Carpets, Woolens, Metalwork, Jewelry, Carvings, and several others. In a small way, Cox and Shielding's did a remarkable diversity of business. Greenwood was the general buyer for the whole business and, with Bessie Smith, was almost indispensable. He pushed open a door at the far end of the passage. This led to the landing of the four-story building, with its floor and steps of stone; there was no lift, and his heels rang out sharply. He stepped into a narrow lane, still cobbled, still with its iron hitching posts, and walked briskly between tall, ugly office buildings to Upper Thames Street, then along another lane to the Monument, where a few tourists stood look-

ing up at the ancient watch tower built to ensure that London
would not burn again. Here cars and vans were parked. An
acquaintance from a shipping company nodded but did not
stop. Greenwood, walking with long strides through the crush
of traffic, the lumbering buses, the mass of pedestrians,
reached the approach to London Bridge.

Shalimar's, an Oriental carpet and curio importing firm, lay
on the other side.

The sun shone warmly, the river surface shimmered, the
dozen ships in the pool of London were all being worked,
booms and cranes and derricks clanged, some holds were
being emptied, some being filled. In the distance, against the
clear blue sky, Tower Bridge looked like an illustration out of
a history book.

Greenwood stood in the middle of London Bridge, staring
down. Ships and buildings and the bridge itself were reflected
in the water, but all he could see was Margaret's face, all he
could hear was Margaret's voice screaming "Eric!" His hands
were tightly clenched, his lips set and thin, his eyes screwed
up. Everywhere he could see and hear her, a never-fading re-
minder of the fact that she was dead.

They had met here, on this bridge, feeding gulls.

He could remember that meeting, over two years ago.

She had been alone on a warm summer's day, lovely, sweet,
and desirable. He would never understand what had happened
to him; how utterly he had surrendered to her attractiveness.
Nor would he understand the absolute nature of her surren-
der to him. It was almost as if on the instant of meeting they
had known that their stars had ordained their union.

Her husband had been away in the tropics, on a three-year
contract with an engineering firm, wives not being allowed on
the project. Their three children had a young woman to take
care of them by day, so that she herself could work.

"I love coming to the City."

"I do, too."

"I always feed the gulls here, winter and summer."

His hand had closed over hers. "I wonder if—"

"Yes?"

"You're free for lunch."

"Oh, how lovely."

Lovely, lovely, lovely. Free for lunch, free for dinner, free
for cinema, theater, supper, free for bed and free for laugh-
ter; free and yet no threat to freedom. They had made a
world of their own, using his bachelor flat in Camberwell,
free from observation, prying eyes, and her husband; always
free. Until Geoffrey Entwistle had come home.

Greenwood felt drawn toward the river's siren call, as if he could hear it whispering, "You have only to come to me, and I will give you rest."

He started, becoming aware of the fact that he had lost count of time. A pleasant-faced young woman was staring at him with some concern. He walked on hurriedly, knowing that she was watching him, well aware of his attractiveness to women. There had been a time when this had been both a satisfaction and an anxiety to him; he had always been afraid of the obligation of love and marriage. With Margaret, he had felt he had everything; then suddenly it had been snatched away from him. He had realized the danger the moment her husband had returned.

At the end of the bridge Greenwood bought an *Evening News* and stood staring down at a photograph of Margaret—lovely Margaret. God! There was a copy of this very photograph at his flat, standing on the radio. Had anyone else seen it? He had no daily help, but—panic rose in him again, driving away the remorse and the grief.

He read:

MOTHER OF THREE STRANGLED

Returning to his Lewisham home last night after a long drive from a business appointment in Leicester, Mr. Geoffrey Entwhistle found his wife's body in the front bedroom.

She had been strangled.

The police are anxious to interview a tall, dark-haired man wearing a light gray suit, who was seen near Number 23, Billitter Street, about eleven fifteen last night. It is believed that Mrs. Entwhistle was murdered between eleven and one o'clock. The killer did not disturb her three sleeping children—Clive, aged 11, Jennifer, 7, and Carol, 4.

Mr. Entwhistle was with the police at Divisional Headquarters between four and seven o'clock, helping with inquiries. Mrs. Entwhistle's mother is looking after the children.

Slowly, Greenwood lowered the newspaper.

He was no longer thinking of Margaret but of his chances of escaping detection. It was ironic that he owed to her the fact that they had always been extremely careful. Almost the only really dangerous move he had made had been that last night at Billitter Street, where he had gone without warning because Margaret had refused to come to him.

If he'd only kept his hands off her, he wouldn't be in this predicament.

How many people *had* seen them together?

Percy Golightly, in charge of a case which already greatly attracted him, was in one of his sunniest moods. He sat at his desk at Scotland Yard with copies of the evening newspapers in front of him. There were excellent pictures of the dead woman and, in one, of her husband and children.

The door opened and a youthful-looking man with a hooked nose came in, carrying a wire tray with photographs. He put this tray on the end of Golightly's desk.

"Two hundred prints, as per your request," he stated.

Golightly picked up the top print, of Greenwood's favorite photograph of a most attractive woman; even he found it hard to believe that she was dead.

"That's good," he said. "Enough for all the Divisions and to spare. Thanks." He nodded dismissal to the man from Photographs and picked up a pencil. He wrote on the back of the photograph, "Accurate likeness of Margaret Entwhistle, murdered by strangulation at 23, Billitter Street, Lewisham, between eleven and one o'clock in the morning, 15/16 of June. M1 Division requests notification if this woman has been seen in the company of any man other than her husband at any time during the past three months (or longer). In emergency also report to Information Room New Scotland Yard or to Chief Superintendent Golightly."

He read this through again, then sent for a sergeant to arrange for it to be duplicated, stuck on the back of the photographs, and distributed. Gideon knew damned well that he would handle the inquiry from this office. Good old Gee-Gee!

Golightly stood up and crossed to a table that held a plastic bag containing dust and lint from the woman's clothing. Pinned to a board were plastic envelopes, containing a number of things: a specimen of her lipstick, her face powder, fingernail scraping, hair—everything that might also be found on her murderer.

Of course, each would almost certainly be found on her husband.

Golightly stood up, whistled softly, went out and upstairs to the laboratory, where white-smocked men stood at a long bench dotted with Bunsen burners and pipettes, test tubes and white crucibles, tripods and forceps. There were two microscopes and all the impedimenta of a reasonably up-to-date chemical laboratory.

"Got something for you," Golightly said to the elderly Superintendent-in-charge.

"Never known the time when you hadn't," the Superintendent said. "This the Entwhistle job?"

"Yes."

"It was the husband, wasn't it?" suggested the laboratory man.

"Who knows?" Golightly asked cryptically.

As this was happening at Scotland Yard, Geoffrey Entwhistle was sitting alone in his house at Billitter Street, Lewisham. His mind was in chaos, grieving and raging at the same time, as well as a little frightened, for he knew that he was under suspicion.

His wife's murderer was at Shalimar's office, discussing a shipment of Tibetan agate. The thief of St. Ludd's was still at Cannon Row Police Station. Gideon was with the Commissioner, discussing Superintendent Alec Hobbs of the C.I.D. At the same time, Superintendent Hugh Rollo was standing in a cellar beneath a house in Fulham, marveling at a collection of nude photographs which really had to be seen to be believed.

"Only time I've ever seen anything like this is in the frescoes at Pompeii," he confided to a sergeant. "The Romans certainly knew how they wanted their lights o' love. My, my. I think I'll bring Gee-Gee along to see this."

His companion, a detective-sergeant of rare temerity, laughed. "If I know Gee-Gee, it won't be the bods he'll want to see, but the photographer who took them."

"Could be. I don't underestimate our commander." Rollo grinned. "He has an artistic eye. First things first, though. Are any of our three dead nudes here? Strictly in the line of duty, Sergeant—take a closer look."

They both laughed, though neither was amused, and began to compare three photographs, each of a murdered girl, with the photographs on the wall. It was a tedious and time-taking business, and during it their jokes were both crude and lewd, yet covered a deadly seriousness.

In his study in an old oak-beamed house near St. Ludd's, the Very Reverend Dean Howcroft was saying into the telephone:

"Yes, I'm quite sure we can rely on his discretion. I was most favorably impressed. . . . No, he hasn't telephoned me yet, but I have a feeling I know whom he will assign to the task. . . . The moment I have any news I will tell you."

CHAPTER 5
RECOMMENDATIONS

Sir Reginald Scott-Marle had been the Commissioner of the Metropolitan Police for several years. Those of his officers who knew him well both liked and respected him. For one thing, he did not pretend to be a detective; he was an administrator. For another, he took advice even in recommending senior appointments, which were made officially by the Home Office. He was aloof to a point of arrogance, but even those who found him cold and distant admitted his scrupulous fairness. Gradually he had become accepted as the true representative of the police, and under his guidance a great number of improvements had been made in working conditions, pay, and general facilities. Members of the Metropolitan Force now felt that they had a square deal, and Gideon, instrumental in persuading Scott-Marle of the need for the improvements, knew that the efficiency of the force was the greater because of the Commissioner.

He reached the door of the Commissioner's office as Scott-Marle, tall, lean, austere-looking, himself turned a corner from the other direction. He nodded and gave a faint smile.

"Good morning, George."

"Good morning, sir."

"Come in." They were as tall as each other, but Gideon was broader than his chief. This was a large office, with a conference room opening out on one side, the secretary's on the other. A telephone bell rang in her room as Scott-Marle motioned to one of two chairs ranged in front of his desk. So only one other was expected.

Hobbs?

One of three telephones on Scott-Marle's desk rang.

"Yes," he said into it. "I see—thank you." He rang off. "Hobbs has been delayed for ten minutes."

"Not your morning for punctuality," Gideon remarked.

"Perhaps that's a good thing, for once. How did Dean Howcroft impress you?"

"Favorably," answered Gideon promptly.

"Good. You had the same effect on him."

Gideon's eyebrows rose. "Has he been in touch with you again?"

"No," said Scott-Marle. Now his smile was, for him, positively broad. "I don't often catch you out in bad staff work."

"Where have I slipped up?" asked Gideon, wary but not embarrassed.

"My wife's brother-in-law is the Bishop," Scott-Marle said, simply.

"Good God! I had no idea, sir." Gideon smiled a little ruefully. "I simply had no idea." As he stared into the Commissioner's amused eyes thoughts were flashing through his mind, and he went on almost without a pause. "If the story's reached the Bishop as quickly as this, the investigation means a lot to them and the problem isn't as simple as the Dean made out."

"Did he make you believe it was simple?"

Gideon said slowly, "I suppose he didn't. He implied that the trouble itself was comparatively trifling, but the task of finding out what was behind it was too complex for the church authorities." Gideon paused, fingering his chin, more perplexed than he liked to admit. "I didn't press him for details—in fact I discouraged him from saying too much."

"He does rather go on and on, doesn't he?" said Scott-Marle. "The trouble is twofold. Minor thefts of the kind which are quite common; and damage which amounts to serious vandalism if it is part of an over-all activity. The anxiety is that either or both could become much more serious. One of the more intractable factors is that the offenses seem to be done by someone with a knowledge of what is most sacred to the churches—they damage things which have ritual significance as well as value, though not, so far, the buildings themselves."

"Hmm," grunted Gideon.

"Have you decided who is to tackle it?"

Gideon hesitated. Then: "I think so," he said.

"Who?"

"Lemaitre."

He could not recall ever seeing Scott-Marle show so much surprise as he did at that answer. He stared at Gideon for a long time, making Gideon wonder whether he would try to dissuade him, even wonder whether his own judgment had been warped by a desire to give Lemaitre's morale a good boost. He did not move in his chair nor shift his gaze.

At last Scott-Marle said, "He's the last man I would have thought of, but I think I see why you're considering him. He will be extremely anxious to succeed, he's a very straightforward fellow with a simple pattern of ethics, he will be shocked by the sacrilege involved but not be impressed by

piety, ritual, or humbug." Scott-Marle paused in the midst of
this quite brilliant assessment of Gideon's thinking, some of it
quite impromptu, and then went on bluntly: "Can we trust his
discretion?"

"I've never had any worry about his discretion," Gideon
said. "He might be too impetuous, but I think he'll restrain
himself over this." Gideon allowed himself a small, experi-
mental grin. "I'll be next door to him all the time, I don't
think that will do any harm."

Scott-Marle shrugged. "There you go, taking on more responsibility than you really should accept. However—I would
certainly like to feel you had this investigation under your
eye. You said you thought you'd decided. Why haven't you
fully made up your mind?"

"Only considered Lemaitre for ten minutes," Gideon
pointed out. "I've decided now, sir."

Scott-Marle said, "Very well. Keep me in close touch,
won't you?" He paused only long enough for Gideon to say,
"I will," before going on without a change of tone. "Now to
the Deputy Commander's post. Have you had any second
thoughts about Hobbs?"

"No."

"None at all?"

"Nothing new," answered Gideon quietly. "He's now had a
full year at N.E. It's been a tough year, and very few men with
his background would have got through it the way he has.
You still get the odd senior officer who sneers about Public
School and party influence, and with a man like Hobbs you
always will. I feared it might prevent him from getting on top
of his job. I don't think so now. I think he'll make a real success of it."

Slowly, thoughtfully, Scott-Marle said, "I hope so, George.
I most certainly hope so. I'm going to recommend him, of
course, and I've no doubt the appointment will be confirmed.
But I'm more troubled than I was before."

"Why, sir?"

Scott-Marle didn't answer at once, and in the pause, movements in the other room suggested that Hobbs had come in.
When a buzzer sounded Scott-Marle pressed a button to tell
his secretary to wait. For the first time since he had entered
the room that day, Gideon saw the other man withdraw,
sensed a cloak of reserve, almost of aloofness, fall upon
him, affecting even the brightness of his eyes. The thing which
most impressed Gideon was the freedom with which he had
talked up to this moment; the change was really a reversion
to normal.

"I want you to give me a serious undertaking," he said very precisely. "If at any time in the next six months you have reason to wonder if the appointment is a success, tell me so. Don't keep it to yourself. I know you take a patriarchal interest in your staff. Don't, please, allow that to influence you about Hobbs. I think he will either be exceptionally good or an unmistakable failure."

Gideon, wondering at the nature of this confidence yet not sharing the doubt, had the sense to say, "I'll keep you informed all along the line, sir."

"Good. Then we'll have him in." In spite of the words, his forefinger hovered over the bell push and there was an almost unfathomable expression in his eyes. "George, I have often wanted to say this to you. I have come to recognize and understand you as a dedicated man. I have known soldiers and sailors, airmen and even politicians with a similar feeling of dedication, but I didn't expect to find it in a policeman. I came to this appointment as an administrator, seeing the Force as another kind of army. In a way, it is. I have come to see it as an instrument in the age-old struggle between good and evil. You have made me regard it so. Try to make Hobbs see it in the same way. He is a very fine detective and an astute man. Intellectually and academically, he is in a class by himself at the Yard. I am not really convinced yet that he has that sense of dedication."

Scott-Marle stopped.

Slowly, almost painfully, Gideon said, "I see what you mean."

He not only saw what the Commissioner meant; he could see why he had doubts about Hobbs. There was another factor which, in other circumstances, might have made him feel self-conscious, but it did not now. He would not have been aware of any sense of dedication in himself. If he had such a sense, it was as natural as breathing, and he didn't think it could be acquired.

If Hobbs hadn't got it, he would probably never have it.

Scott-Marle said, "All right, George," and pressed the bell push.

Chief Superintendent Alec Hobbs was almost too short for a policeman, barely above the regulation five feet eight inches. There was something curiously controlled about him—the way he dressed, the way he spoke and looked, the way he moved. His clothes, impeccably tailored, were a shade too formal, and every suit he wore appeared to be an exact replica of the last. His dark hair, graying slightly at the temples, was always exactly the same; he had it trimmed every ten days. He had been educated at Repton and King's College, Cambridge, and had spent a year at one of the major American universities—Gideon could never remember which. There had at one time been a certain amount of prejudice against him as being Old School Tie, but as Gideon knew, this intense jealousy had mostly vanished.

He had a private income but no one knew how much. He lived expensively but without ostentation in a flat overlooking the river at Chelsea with his invalid wife, to whom he was devoted and with whom he spent all of his spare time. She was —or she had been—a very beautiful woman, but in recent months her looks had faded, as if her illness were eating them away.

This was the man whom Gideon, a product of a London elementary and secondary school education, had recommended as his deputy; and almost certainly the man who would one day step into Gideon's shoes.

That morning he moved toward the Commissioner's office, guessing, without being absolutely sure, of the reason for his summons. Gideon shifted in his seat without rising; Scott-Marle motioned to the one empty chair. Hobbs knew instinctively that they had been discussing him: well, why not? Scott-Marle's expression gave nothing away and Gideon looked a little preoccupied. Hobbs believed he understood Gideon more, in fact, than he understood Scott-Marle, who was first and last a soldier as Hobbs understood soldiers.

"I hope you weren't delayed by anything serious," Scott-Marle said. Reproof was implicit in his words.

"Traffic, sir," Hobbs said, half truthfully. He had never been able to talk freely about his wife and could not bring himself to say that it was a specialist who had been delayed on a visit to her, not he himself.

Scott-Marle made no comment, but continued smoothly. "I would like to recommend your appointment as Deputy Commander of the Criminal Investigation Department, Hobbs. Can I do so with the certainty of your acceptance should the post be offered?"

Outwardly, Hobbs was unmoved. Inwardly, he exulted. "Yes, sir, you can. Thank you."

"You have Gideon to thank as much if not more than I," Scott-Marle declared.

He glanced at Gideon, who felt a sudden sense of need to put Hobbs at his ease. Scott-Marle, having let himself go so much this morning, was instinctively stiffening again, and the familiar cold exterior was already very faintly hostile. If the conversation could not be lightened, it could at least be changed.

He said adroitly, "Have you heard about the trouble at St. Ludd's?"

"An old lag has been arrested, hasn't he?" There was very little that missed Hobbs.

"Yes, but there's more to it than that. The Dean——"

"Howcroft?"

"Yes. Do you know him?"

"Yes. Socially."

"He's worried about what he calls minor offenses in a lot of churches and cathedrals," Gideon said. "He wants us to probe, without making it obvious what we're doing."

"Using the thief as the ostensible reason for the St. Ludd's investigation," Hobbs divined. "It must be serious, or he wouldn't come to us." He broke off, obviously waiting for some further comment. Scott-Marle was simply watching them, taking all this in but being no help at all. Gideon pondered before saying almost sententiously, "Who would you put in charge of that, Alec?"

He hoped the "Alec" would lighten the atmosphere, yet was uneasy because, if Hobbs was socially a friend of the Dean, he might have some reservations about Lemaitre. These *bloody* politics! Gideon had no time for them at all and almost resented Scott-Marle's decision to consult him. Hobbs, frowning very slightly, still determined not to show any feeling, was thinking fast. At last he shifted his position slightly, and said, "Lemaitre, I think, if you can spare him from his desk."

Thank God for that! thought Gideon.

If anything was calculated to show that Hobbs had a heart as well as a head, this was it. He chuckled and Scott-Marle visibly relaxed. Hobbs knew that he had said the right thing.

Sally Dalby was a long way from sure that she was right; in fact she was afraid she had both spoken and acted unwisely, but she did not see how she could get out of it now. She sat alone in a cubicle in a cellar in North London, half undressed, nervous, and ashamed. She heard Toni Bottelli moving about in the main part of the cellar, and she could hear the background music of a radio. Everything seemed so ordinary and normal, yet here she was, actually undressing so that a man she hardly knew could take her photograph.

"I'm just a prude," she muttered to herself; then almost at once she thought, what would Dad say? She unrolled one stocking as far as the beautifully soft and rounded calf of her leg, but stopped suddenly. *"I can't do it!"* She spoke very clearly and precisely. On impulse she rolled the stocking up, snatched her skirt from a hook and drew it on, zipped it with an almost feverish motion, and stretched out for her blouse. She had it half on, arms thrust backward into the sleeves, bosom thrust forward, when the man she hardly knew pulled the curtain aside roughly and demanded:

"How long are you going to be?"

It was the expression on his handsome face, far more than his words or his manner, which touched her with fear.

CHAPTER 6
CHILD IN TERROR

Toni Bottelli stood glaring at Sally, and suddenly she felt worse than naked: she felt besmirched. His expression changed from impatience and anger to lustful gloating; she could not mistake that for an instant. She backed away but there was so little space, and her hands knocked painfully against the wall.

Bottelli raised his eyebrows. "Take your time."

"Toni, go away."

"What a hope!"

"Leave me alone, I want to get dressed!"

"You've got the wrong idea, Sally old gel. You want to get undressed."

"No, I—I won't! I can't!"

"You *can't?*" mocked Toni, and there was a harsher note in his voice. "I'll help you, if you like."

"Get away from me!"

As she stood there in terror she had no idea how beautiful she looked, with her honey-brown eyes shining with that fear, the long lashes curling against her fair skin, stained now with a defiant flush. Her lips were parted, and her teeth just showed; she was on the verge of shivering. All she knew was that she was desperately afraid of him. She was seventeen, and although she had known the exploring fingers of youths of her own age, she was a virgin, with all a virgin's dread of violence; yet this man's will to violence showed in his very face, in the tautness of his body. An older woman or an experienced one would have taken one glance at him and warned: "Don't trust him an inch."

If he lays a hand on me, she thought, I'll die.

She did not, she could not, know how true that might be. She simply sensed some horrible and impending danger.

Her shallow breathing reached a climax and she began to gulp and gasp. She was aware of it and was now frightened by the feeling of suffocation, knowing that she had to move away, that her body was going limp, her legs beginning to tremble. She thought hysterically: why doesn't he *do* something, why does he just stay there?

Being so young, she did not notice the almost imperceptible change in his expression, the way the glitter in his eyes began to fade, or the way the taut muscles at his lips relaxed. Now the screaming of her nerves and the choking difficulty of her breathing brought her to the verge of collapse. Her lips began to quiver, her teeth to chatter, quite beyond control.

Suddenly, Bottelli said, "Relax, baby."

She hardly heard him.

"Relax," he repeated, and moved to take a robe of gay toweling from a peg on the wall. "Put that on. I'm not going to touch you."

She could hardly believe what he was saying.

"Take it easy." He backed away a pace, holding the gown out for her to put on. When she did not move, baffled by the change in him, he tossed it at her and moved away. "What you need is a drink," he said over his shoulder.

A tremendous sense of gratitude flowed through her, of release, as if some drug had been injected into her veins and was moving through her blood stream, warming, soothing. His back was toward her. She shrugged the shirt-blouse on, the buttons defeating her unsteady hands, pulling the robe tight, tying the sash. There was a couch against one wall, the only one not covered with photographs. As she moved toward it, her legs still weak, she heard the chink of glasses. When she dropped down, Bottelli turned round, holding two glasses. Walking toward her, he was the man she had first met and thought so handsome, with his beautiful black hair and his olive skin, his luminous dark eyes set against black lashes and brows. He was rather small, but beautifully formed, which was particularly obvious because he wore only a dark, short-sleeved shirt and faded jeans.

He stood over her, holding out a glass.

"Here's to you," he said.

She took the glass and sipped. It was whisky. Suddenly it flashed through her mind that drinking whisky so early in the day was a very dashing, grown-up thing to do, and she felt a little giggle rising within her.

"Here's to *you*," she said.

"That's my Sally!"

They both drank, more deeply.

"What got into you?" he asked, and his manner, his tone of voice, everything about him had changed; she was aware of it without even beginning to understand.

"I—I don't know, Toni."

"Scared of me?"

"Course I wasn't!"

"You don't have to be."

"I know I don't."

He lowered himself to the edge of the couch, beside her.

"You never will have to be scared of me."

"I know," she repeated.

"Not now, or ever." He sipped, and gave a little quirk of a smile, a most attractive one, the kind which would have lulled the suspicions of many an experienced woman, and melted the resistance of most others.

Sally looked puzzled, in her naïve and simple way.

"What do you mean—not *now?*"

"What I say, Sally."

"You mean—" her eyes looked enormous—"I did have reason to be scared of you?"

"You certainly did."

"I—I don't understand you."

His smile, so attractive and winsome, became much wider.

"Take a look in the mirror," he said.

After a moment's pause she caught the meaning of the compliment, and gave a pleased little laugh.

"Don't give me that!"

"Go on, look in the mirror. There's one on the wall."

She looked round at the array of photographs, which had shocked her when she had first come in, making her nervous and starting the tension which had brought her to revolt. There was no sign of a mirror, although she knew there was a small one in the cubicle.

"What wall?" she asked.

"Don't believe me, eh?" Toni scoffed.

In the nicest possible way he patted her knee, got up, and crossed to the wall opposite the cubicle. It appeared to be a solid mass of photographs and she colored a little, because some of them were in peculiar poses. There was one of a girl, naked, back to the camera, legs apart, bending down and peering between them, long hair falling almost to the floor.

Sally did not want to look too closely at this or any of the others, deciding comfortably that most of them were no worse than the colored photographs one could see on the bookstalls in the West End, remarkable for outsized breasts and tiny waists.

"Here you are," Toni said brightly.

He put out a hand, pulled at a small knob which she hadn't noticed, and a section of the wall folded back revealing a full-length mirror. With a start of surprise she saw herself in the colorful gown, fair hair a little untidy, even the fringe out of place, eyes starry and cheeks flushed.

"Now you have to admit, that's something," Toni Bottelli said.

"Oh, go on!"

"I knew you had something the first moment I set eyes on you," he declared. "I'm more than a photographer, *they're* two-a-penny. I'm an artist, too. Got an artist's eye for a figure, and it takes more than a blouse and skirt to fool me. You want to know something? I've been an artist photographer for nine years, and in my considered opinion I've never seen *anyone* with a better figure than yours."

That pleased her greatly, but she protested.

"You've never even *seen* it."

"I can tell."

"You're just flattering me."

"What's wrong with a bit of flattery, Sal?" He slid his arm round her waist and squeezed, then moved away toward a camera which stood on a tripod at one end of the room. Opposite this was a raised platform, draped in black, and two silken cushions, beautifully colored; beyond it a low stool with an iridescent cover of pale sea-greens. "I know I'm right, though."

"I'll bet you say the same thing to every girl who comes in here."

"Oh, well," said Toni, off-handedly, "if you don't want to believe that I think you've got the most beautiful body I've ever come across, I can't make you. And I certainly don't want to take your photograph if you don't want me to. Get dressed and buzz, baby! I've got to get myself another model."

He began to whistle.

Sally went into the cubicle and stood very still for a few seconds, piqued and even annoyed at the sudden change in Toni's manner, yet still intrigued and flattered by his compliments. Near her were several photographs in black and white of quite lovely girls; there was no doubt of the artistry in the pose and the shadows, they *were* beautiful. If she was better than they were, it was really something. Toni ought to know if he had taken all of these pictures. Why, there must be thousands! And he *was* an artist, everyone knew that artists were used to seeing models in the nude; what was it her mother sometimes said? In the altogether. Funny old Mum! And Toni couldn't have been nicer; once he had realized that she was worried, he had been ever so understanding. She must have been quite wrong about him.

Her eyes lit up as decision came upon her. She stripped off the robe, then her blouse and bra, then her stockings and belt. Soon she stood naked, except that a tiny gold chain and cross were about her neck—a gift from her mother, two birthdays ago.

She hesitated; then unfastened the chain, slipped it off and put it in her handbag. Excitement had bubbled out of her fear. She moved back and studied the photographs in the cubicle to select a pose which seemed to set the model's body off best; one hand on her hip, one just covering the nipple of her breast, head tilted backward. She practiced several times, aware of movements in the studio, another *ting* of a telephone. Suddenly she realized that Toni might really be sending for another model. Thrusting the curtains aside cautiously, she stepped out. He was still busy on the telephone, sideways to her, talking in earnest undertones. She crept toward the platform, watching him, but he seemed not to notice. She stepped onto it and struck the pose, with only a momentary qualm.

That did not strike her as strange. Her heart was light, and she felt quite exhilarated as she gave what she hoped was a professional model's smile. Toni replaced the telephone and glanced up.

He gaped.

The effect was exactly what she had hoped for: staggering. My, how handsome he was! Sitting there, looking upward across the room, lips parted, eyes rounded. After what seemed a long time, he let out a long, slow breath.

"Was I right," he breathed, so that she could just hear. "*Was* I."

He began to stand up, slowly.

She felt wonderful; wonderful.

"Am I all right?"

"*Are* you! I knew it—the moment I set eyes on you I knew it, you've got the most beautiful body I've ever seen in a woman." He moved slowly forward, his gaze raking her and finally coming to rest in the valley between her breasts—

where the cross had rested. "You're going to be the most fa-
mous model in London," he promised her. "Now, I know exactly the right pose for you. Not that one, you want one made
especially for you. Posing a model is like being a choreogra-
pher, you know—arranging a ballet. That's what you are,
really, a ballet of the body." He climbed up onto the platform
and put his hands on her arms. "Now, let's see. I think I'd like
you reclining. That's right, reclining." He exerted sufficient
pressure to make her lean backward, but he supported her.
"I've got to get you in a dozen positions, first, to make sure
which is the best."

The strange thing was, she did not mind his hands.

Soon, she was reclining. He left her, fetched a camera with
a close-up lens and began to take pictures from all angles, all
positions. Now and again he would pause to adjust her position, and she held whatever pose he made for her. Finally he
allowed her to relax on her back, the cushions arching her
body slightly. . . .

When he came to her, she was nearly asleep; drowsy,
happy, aware of what was happening and yet oblivious, too.

In the cellar at Fulham, on the other side of London, Hugh
Rollo was saying to the knowing sergeant:

"None of the three we're after, then. That's a pity."

"Can't have all the luck," remarked the sergeant.

"No reason why we shouldn't hope for it," said Rollo. He
spoke absently as he moved about the studio, glancing at the
photographs as a mass, now, not individually. "We counted
over a thousand. How many different faces?"

"Thirty-two."

"Thirty-two," echoed Rollo. "And two out of three taken in
a pose that would get anyone who published them locked up
for obscenity."

"*Or* exhibited them for profit," remarked the sergeant
smugly.

"Notice anything else?" asked Rollo.

"They're good photographs."

"Not that. A common factor."

The sergeant grinned. "Female form divine," he suggested.

"Age," prompted Rollo.

"Age?"

"Late teens, middle teens."

The sergeant frowned and began to look again; after a few
seconds, he said, "Now you come to mention it, yes. There
aren't any older women here—all young girls." He scowled
suddenly, angrily. "*I've* got two teen-age daughters."

Slowly, Rollo said, "I don't know whether I have, but Gee
—" he paused and corrected: "Gideon has. Just about make
him mad, this will."

"What will?"

Rollo said: "I'll tell the Commander what I think, you work
it out for yourself. There are two things," the Superintendent
went on. "They're right under your nose. Don't miss 'em."

CHAPTER 7
GIDEON PROPOSES . . .

Gideon was in a much livelier and more normal frame of
mind that afternoon. Some of his problems had been resolved,
several decisions had been made, leaving his mind free to
cope with the new cases which were going through. So that he
could have time to concentrate, he did not tell Lemaitre all
that had been decided when he left the Commissioner's office,
but simply said, "It's Hobbs," and went into his own office.
He had some slight misgivings about Hobbs's motive in recommending Lemaitre; it *could* have been out of a sense of
humanity and good will, it might have been because he gen-
uinely felt Lemaitre to be the right man, and it could possibly
be that Hobbs thought it would please him, Gideon.

Gideon turned to the reports on his desk. Two more had
come in, and there was a request from Golightly: "Spare me
ten minutes this afternoon, if you can."

Gideon made a note to send for him at half-past three.
Then he lost himself in the cases that were being investigated,
the ever increasing volume and the ever increasing variety of
crime. Discounting those crimes induced by new and irritating
laws which were not his to question, most of the increase
seemed to him to be due to three causes, at least one of them
seldom considered in the sociological surveys and reports.

There were more people: the same crime ratio for a population figure of forty million inevitably meant more actual
crimes in a population of over fifty million. A five percent increase in crime in ten years was hardly an increase at all.

There were too few police: the establishment of every force
in the country was below strength, some of them seriously.
Here at the Yard the Criminal Investigation Department establishment wasn't too bad; they could use more but were no

longer seriously undermanned. The uniformed branch was, however; and the deterrent and preventive effect of the policeman on his beat or in a patrol car still could not be calculated, although it was very important indeed.

There was the third major factor which only a fool could ignore: the actual increase in crime because more and more people were prepared to rob their neighbors. Even if one made every allowance for the first two factors, this third was the most significant and the most ominous. More people were cold-bloodedly prepared to break the law; and while by far the greater proportion of criminals were the old lags and the professionals who were mostly unintelligent and habitual, there was this new breed to contend with: the clever criminal who planned not only his crimes but the disposal of his loot and his way of life, so that capturing him was extremely difficult. There were not a great number of these men, but they took up the time of the police out of all proportion to their numbers. Below this intellectual level of criminals there were still many more prepared to live a life of crime for its own sake. The majority of these appeared to be the products of a welfare state which had created living standards the lack of which the social pundits had once believed to be the basic cause of crime.

In the old days, when the Bow Street Runners had been formed and Fielding had wielded both influence and power, most crimes had been committed out of desperate need. In the present time, most were committed out of greed and the desire for an easy life, or out of some neurotic or psychopathic factor that found in crime the thrill of excitement or a sadistic pleasure in violence and pain. This was the ugliest aspect, and one against which Gideon had steadfastly fought; he simply did not want to believe that some of the worst instincts of man asserted themselves in a modern society.

But they did. No one could dispute that there was much more evil in crime than there had been.

Now, going through the reports, he found himself seeing each case in the light of this new thinking, aware that Scott-Marle was largely responsible for it. There was a week-old murder investigation—a girl raped, mutilated, strangled. Beastly but not new, commonplace in many parts of the world long before Jack the Ripper had frightened half the women of London. So far, there was no clue to the killer. Next, a post office holdup in which a woman had been attacked when trying to call the police; not uncommon, either. Third, a case of an old man, penniless, set upon by half a dozen youths and beaten to the point of death. Ugh! Savagery. One of the "new" types of crime. The three young girls, poisoned. No one knew why, no one had any idea by whom; but Gideon, highly sensitive, was afraid that before long the body of a fourth might be found—perhaps tomorrow, which meant that tomorrow's corpse would be today's living, vital body. Of all the cases, Gideon was most troubled by this. There was the murder of Mrs. Entwhistle, a commonplace enough crime. And there were the church "offenses."

It was time he told Lemaitre about that assignment.

He made a few notes and pushed the pile of reports away from him; as he did so, the interoffice telephone bell rang.

"Gideon."

"Can you see Golightly soon?" asked Lemaitre.

"Yes. Where is he?"

"In my office."

"Send him in," ordered Gideon. "Wait a minute, though, make a note of this while I think of it. We could do with a consultant on freak or fringe religious sects—there must be some specialists about. Find one."

"Okay, George," Lemaitre promised.

Gideon put down the receiver as another telephone bell rang. He picked up the receiver again impatiently.

"Gideon."

"Will you speak to Superintendent Rollo, sir?"

"Yes." Gideon saw Golightly come in, and waved to a chair. He was opening the Entwhistle murder file as Hugh Rollo's voice sounded in his ear.

"Can you spare me twenty minutes, Commander?"

"When?"

"Any time you like."

"Four o'clock," Gideon said. "We'll have a cup of tea in my office." He rang off and gave his familiar half-rueful smile to Golightly. "Made an arrest yet, Percy?"

"Not yet," said Golightly, in a slightly guarded voice.

"Anywhere near?"

"I wouldn't be surprised—" the Superintendent's tone conveyed an ambiguity that might be hiding a tenuous but jealously held clue, or might, on the other hand, merely cover a cunning hope that Gideon would think so—"if the husband isn't our man."

Gideon made no comment but remembered Lemaitre's jumping to the same easy belief in the husband's guilt. He would be elated if it did indeed prove to be the answer.

"Geoffrey Entwhistle has been away for three years—only home for a couple of weeks each Christmas. A neighbor told him that his wife was often out in the evenings. Wifey—"

"The dead woman?"

"Yes," said Golightly, taking the implied rebuke in his stride. "She left home two or three times a week, looking radiant—"

"Whose word?" asked Gideon.

"A neighbor's."

"The neighbor?"

"The original talebearer, plus three others we've questioned today. Moreover Margaret Entwhistle was seen in nightclubs with a man—the same man—fairly frequently. Entwhistle received an anonymous letter just before coming home, telling him about this. He *says* he didn't tackle his wife about it; that he was no saint himself when away from home, and that he was as much in love with her as ever."

"Any evidence?" Gideon asked.

"At least one terrific quarrel with her, two days ago."

"Who told you?"

"Two neighbors and the eldest child, a boy of eleven. George," went on Golightly, his lips curving, "I am not doing a Lem on you." Gideon grunted. "Entwhistle went home at eleven o'clock last night. He left Leicester at half past seven, came down on the M1 motorway and reached Lewisham just before eleven. His Jaguar two-and-a-half litre was seen by a Divisional policeman. Two neighbors saw him go into the house, then come out very agitated a little before twelve o'clock. He drove off from the car park at the end of Billitter Street and didn't get in touch with us until after three o'clock. All of these things can be proved to the hilt. In a way, I wish they couldn't."

Gideon pursed his lips. "Then why haven't you charged Entwhistle?"

"I wanted to see what you thought. I know you don't like circumstantial evidence."

"From what you say," temporized Gideon, "this is the strongest circumstantial evidence we'll ever get."

"I think it is."

"But you're still doubtful," Gideon said. "You want to pass the buck."

Golightly frowned a little; his voice softened disarmingly.

"You really do know me, George, don't you?" It was the second time that day that Golightly had dropped into the familiar "George," although there was an unwritten law that familiarity should not be encouraged on duty. "I'm far from sure about Entwhistle. It looks black but—" He broke off.

"You have a feeling," Gideon said dryly. From any other senior policeman the remark would have been derisory.

Golightly looked faintly like a boy caught out in a misdemeanor.

"Yes. I have a feeling. It looks right, it feels wrong."

It would be easy to ask why, but impossible for Golightly to explain. It would be a grave mistake to ridicule the feeling, too; many a good detective had a nose for the truth. Gideon contemplated the rather blank-looking Superintendent for some time before saying, "Bring Entwhistle here for questioning, and I'll have a look at him. If he doesn't want to come, charge him. Tell the press—" He broke off, suddenly shocked, for the word "press" reminded him that he had promised a statement to the newspapermen about the Cathedral robbery but had forgotten. He made a penciled note, grunted, "Reminded me of something," and went on. "Tell the press he's being held, and encourage them to think we suspect him. Then if there *is* a lover—"

"No doubt about that," interpolated Golightly.

"Well, in that case the lover might—if he is guilty—give himself up," Gideon said. "It's one thing to commit a murder and quite another to let an innocent man swing for it."

"But they don't swing these days," Golightly corrected gloomily.

"Metaphorically they do," said Gideon crisply. He wondered if it was expecting too much, or not enough, of the murderer. A practiced criminal, a professional, might stand by and allow another man to be charged for a crime he had committed, but an ordinary citizen who had committed a crime was not likely to. The tension of waiting, the burden of guilt, usually impelled such a man to make some admission— sometimes by giving himself up and confessing, as often by writing or telephoning anonymously to the police or a newspaper. But it was by no means automatic. Gideon ruminated over what had been said. In any case, he would soon be able to form an opinion of Entwhistle himself.

"What about the children?" he asked.

"Still with grandma."

"Seen them?" asked Gideon.

"Yes. That's how I heard about the quarrel. The eleven-year-old had told his grandmother and she told me."

"The wife's mother?" Gideon inquired.

"Yes. And she can't wait to see the son-in-law who deserted her daughter for three years charged with the murder. No love there, George."

Gideon said wryly, "So I see."

Golightly, reading dismissal in the air, pushed his chair back and stood up. Gideon watched him go, then lifted the telephone and asked for the Back Room Inspector. When the man came on the line, Gideon said, "There's nothing special about the St. Ludd's theft for the press. Tell 'em so, will you?"

"Yes, sir."

Gideon rang off and crossed to the window, looking out onto a troubled Thames. The sun had gone, clouds were low, the wind was high. It looked almost wintry. He pushed up a window as Big Ben began to strike four, and he thought regretfully that when they were in the new building he would miss Big Ben. He heard the door open, knew it was Rollo, but did not look round immediately. The door closed. Rollo did not call out but moved to the desk rather stealthily; he was in some ways the most self-confident man at the Yard, and no respecter of persons. What was he up to? When Gideon turned, Rollo was swiveling round at the desk, smiling.

"Good afternoon," he said.

"What's it all about?" asked Gideon.

"A kind of guessing game," said Rollo.

"I don't much like guessing."

"I'd be glad if you would have a look at these, though." Rollo motioned to a dozen or so photographs which he had laid out on the desk, and Gideon went across; there was no particular reason for discouraging him.

Each photograph was of the head, shoulders, and bosom of a girl. Each girl, in her way, was attractive; some were beautiful. Some were dark, some fair. All were quite remarkably well-developed, all posed so as to show their breasts to fullest advantage. As far as Gideon could judge the nipples had not been touched up; these were natural.

"What's the question?" he asked.

"The common denominator," Rollo said.

It would not be the obvious one—sex; but nor would it be particularly subtle, being posed by Rollo. Smothering a laugh, Rollo produced a dozen more photographs, laying them out with great precision. Except that each was of a different girl, they were almost identical. Size, he wondered? Bust measurement? Age? *Age*. They were all very young, very well-developed for their age, which was probably in the middle teens.

"Age," he said. "Sixteen, seventeen? And the same dark background."

Rollo almost guffawed. "Trust you," he said. "Right on the spot. Commander, I found one thousand and ten photographs round the walls of that cellar, and these are the nicest of them. Some of the others are obscene by almost any standard. There were thirty-two different models in all, each one young, no known professional models or prostitutes among them. Our three dead nudes would fit in the pattern easily. Their photographs weren't included, but could well have been. What's more, these are all prints. I couldn't find a single plate or negative—and I couldn't find any duplicates, either. See what I'm driving at?"

"Other cellars, full of them," hazarded Gideon.

Rollo was startled. "Er—well, yes. I was really thinking of the original cellar or studio, where these were taken. You've noticed the little speck in the corner of each background, and there's a good chance they were all taken at the same place. I'd like to charge the chemist's assistant who developed these under the Obscene Publications Act, and talk to him."

"What's stopping you?" asked Gideon, momentarily exasperated; had every senior officer chosen today to evade his responsibility?

"He's packed up and left his lodgings," Rollo said simply. "This wouldn't normally be a charge with a general call but I'd like to see him as soon as I can."

"Put out the call and the description," Gideon ordered, abruptly. He went on almost as if talking to himself. "A lot of young girls, a lot of nasty poses, good pay or some kind of inducement or persuasion—they all seem happy enough—in fact they look very dreamy, don't they?"

"George," said Chief Superintendent Rollo, the second man to break the unwritten law of names and titles that day, "I really do hand it to you. Dreamy is the word. So you see the common denominator and why I want that chap pulled in."

"You're afraid that drugs are being used."

"Could be."

"Get him," said Gideon. "I don't like that possibility at all." He moved to the desk, sorted through some of the files, took out those on the photo-nude murders, and read through the summary: "Clear indications of (purple hearts) in each blood sample. Dose not large. Probably taken within an hour of death." "Yes," he went on. "Get these devils quickly."

He thought again of the dread possibility that some young girl, lovely and full of life and as beautiful as any of these, might be the next victim of the same murderer.

Such as Sally Dalby.

CHAPTER 8
FRIGHTENED MAN

Geoffrey Entwhistle was a very frightened man.

He recognized himself as being in the grip of a web of circumstantial evidence which already almost precluded a chance of escape. Fighting for his life, he was shocked to discover that in his deep concern for himself there was hardly a thought in his mind for Meg or his children. Meg was dead and the children were in the care of a woman who disliked him but would do her duty by them—whereas his own problem was terribly urgent and pressing.

He sat in a bleak, bare room at Scotland Yard, where he had been for over half an hour. Standing by the door was a youthful-looking man in plain clothes; outside was a policeman in uniform. There were a table, two hard wood chairs, and a Bible; that was peculiar, a Bible. No one spoke to him, but on the desk was a newspaper, the *Evening Echo,* with a photograph of Meg.

The door opened sharply enough to make him jump. The detective who had already questioned him twice came in, alone. He was a little too smooth, a little too honey-tongued. In this gloomy room, his eyes seemed full of menacing shadows. He closed the door behind him as Entwhistle stood up.

"You may sit down."

Entwhistle dropped back into his chair. It was too small for him, for he was a tall, bony man, his cheeks pale with the pallor of the tropics, his aquiline features sharpened by anxiety. His eyes were tired, and the lids drooped.

"I want to ask you some questions," Golightly said.

Entwhistle said wearily, "*More* questions? I tell you I know nothing about my wife's death."

"If you don't, you have nothing to fear," said Golightly.

The bloody fool! thought Entwhistle, ivory pallor flushing in powerless anger. I know nothing about it and yet there's a hell of a risk that I'll be found guilty of murder. Isn't *that* enough cause for fear?

Golightly, seeing the color suffuse his cheeks, made a mental note: that Entwhistle was truly frightened.

51

"This time," said Golightly, "we are going to take questions and answers down in shorthand. Have you any objection?"

"No." Get on with it, thought Entwhistle.

"Did you kill your wife?"

"No."

"Did you return home at about eleven fifteen last night?"

"Yes."

"Did you leave again about an hour later?"

"Yes."

"Did you report the death of your wife at three o'clock this morning?"

"Yes."

"Did you untruthfully state that you had returned home at three o'clock, found her dead, and then telephoned the police?"

"Yes."

"Why did you lie?"

"I—I don't know."

Without a change of tone, without the slightest hind of impatience, Golightly asked again:

"Why did you lie?"

"I still don't know."

"Was your wife alive when you arrived home at eleven o'clock?"

"No."

"Are you sure?"

"Yes."

"How can you be sure?"

"I held a mirror in front of her lips, tried her pulse, and felt for her heart. There was no sign of life. I gave her the kiss of life, without success."

"Are you a qualified physician?"

"No, but I am fully trained in first aid."

"When and where were you trained?"

"In London, before taking up my appointment in Siam. Becoming fully proficient in first aid was a condition of the appointment." Entwhistle answered almost automatically. "I took a twelve-month part-time course with the St. John Ambulance Brigade and have their certificate."

"Thank you. And you are quite sure your wife was dead?" Entwhistle drew a deep breath. *"Yes."*

"Did you telephone for a doctor?"

"No."

"Why not?"

"I saw no point in doing so."

"Why didn't you notify the police?"

Wearily, Entwhistle answered, "I *still* don't know. I suppose I was in a state of shock. I couldn't really believe it."

"What precisely do you mean by 'it'?"

"That my wife was dead."

"Thank you. What *did* you do on making this tragic discovery?"

"I went to see my children. They were all asleep, and obviously they didn't know anything was wrong."

"Thank you. What did you do after seeing if the children were all right?"

"I wanted to think. I just went out."

"Leaving the children to wake and find their mother dead?"

Entwhistle did not answer the question, but stared intently at Golightly, as if at some new kind of anatomical specimen; and the detective kept silent, perhaps because Entwhistle's expression affected him.

"Let *me* ask a question," Entwhistle said. "Have you any children?"

"No, but the question is immaterial."

"I think not," said Entwhistle brusquely. "If you had children, you would know that little short of an earthquake would wake them at dead of night, once they were asleep. There wasn't a chance of them finding their mother."

"So when you left, you intended to return before long."

Entwhistle said gruffly, "I suppose I took it for granted that I would. I just walked. I couldn't even tell you where I went —I just had to keep on the move."

"Mr. Entwhistle, saying that you suppose you took your return for granted is hardly an answer to the question," Golightly observed. "Did you intend to return or not?"

"I—I suppose so."

"Why did you leave at all?"

"I was so—so shocked. I wanted to think."

"Do you think it normal for a man who comes in and finds his wife murdered to need to go out and *think* before deciding that he should telephone the police, send for a doctor, and also send for someone to look after his children?"

Entwhistle said bleakly, "I should think normality hardly came into it. In such a situation a man does not have much practice. You must take it from me that *I* needed to think."

"Why?"

"The whole thing knocked me cold."

"Mr. Entwhistle," Golightly said, "it is not unknown for a husband to have good reason to be jealous of his wife, to have cause for bitterness and resentment. Did *you* have any reason to be jealous of your wife?"

Entwhistle's forehead was shiny with sweat, and there was a fractional pause before he answered, "I've told you already! I'm not the jealous type!"

"I would like you to tell me again, for the record," said Golightly, glancing at the plain-clothes man, who was making his notes with effortless ease, hardly pausing except when there was a much longer gap than usual between question and answer. "Had you reason to be jealous?"

"I had a filthy letter from some damned busybody, probably a woman who didn't know what she was talking about. It made all kinds of accusations. I knew where to put *that*."

"Did you believe the accusations, Mr. Entwhistle?"

"I've told you before—I don't give a damn what people say. I'm no plaster saint myself. My wife was on her own for three years, with the kids to look after, and if she had some companionship, male, *I* wouldn't blame her. In fact I'd rather she was happy with someone else than sitting miserable at home by herself, wishing she were dead."

"What makes you think she would have wished she were dead?" flashed Golightly.

"That was a figure of speech."

"In the circumstances, a very sinister one," Golightly rasped.

As he spoke, the door opened and another, much bigger man came in. Entwhistle had the feeling that he had seen him before, but couldn't place him. Golightly jumped up and the plain-clothes man sprang to attention, so this was a V.I.P. There was something about the rugged face and the penetrating gray eyes beneath rather shaggy eyebrows which impressed Entwhistle.

"Good evening, Commander," said Golightly. "This is Mr. Geoffrey Entwhistle. Mr. Entwhistle, this is Commander Gideon."

Ah! Gideon.

Gideon, to Entwhistle's surprise, shook hands; his grip was very powerful. His gaze was searching, even disconcerting, and against him Golightly faded into insignificance. The sergeant brought another chair for Gideon, who sat down. When they were all seated, he said dryly, "I heard that unfortunate figure of speech. Go on from there, Superintendent."

"That's all it was," Entwhistle said sharply, his voice slightly higher than normal.

"So you said," murmured Gideon.

That was the moment when Entwhistle's spirits dropped, when he felt the net really closing in. There was no justification at all for their suspicions of him; but who would believe it? It was his own fault, his innocent folly, the way he had behaved last night with never a thought to safeguard his position. Didn't these coppers understand what could happen to a man who came in and found his wife dead, murdered? What harm had the delay in reporting her death done to *her*?

Golightly said in a subdued voice: "Mr. Entwhistle has somewhat unconventional attitudes towards marital fidelity, Commander. He was told anonymously that his wife had a lover, but (a) refused to believe it and (b) said that he himself being no saint, had no right to do other than expect her to amuse herself in her own way. Is that correct, Mr. Entwhistle?"

"I think I'll have the question and answer verbatim," Gideon said.

There was a pause as he looked espectantly at the shorthand notes. The plain-clothes man flipped over a page, collected himself, and began to read in a heavy, expressionless voice of deadly monotony. Every word was enunciated carefully, everything was verbatim, but as Entwhistle heard, his heart went cold within him. He knew exactly how his words, without his own inflections, struck Gideon; how heartless and improbable they sounded. He watched Gideon's face and saw the way his expression hardened and bleakness touched his eyes.

The stenographer finished.

Gideon nodded, and said, "Was your wife aware of your attitude toward such matters, Mr. Entwhistle?"

"I doubt it."

"Don't you know?"

"It's hardly a subject I would discuss with her, is it?" asked Entwhistle. Try as he might, he could not keep a cold, half-sneering tone out of his voice, and knew that almost every word strengthened the bad impression he was making. The worst thing was his inability to explain what had driven him away from the house last night. How could he explain what he could not explain to himself? It had been like coming home to a nightmare, going off had been a kind of effort to wake himself up. . . . And yet in another way he had simply run from the hideous reality, not wanting to admit the truth.

"Did you know your wife's lover?" Golightly demanded.

"I've told you, I don't even know that she had one!"

"Did you have any reason to suspect she had a lover before you left England three years ago?" Golightly's merciless voice did not change tone or expression as his questions went on and on.

"What do you make of him?" Golightly asked Gideon.

"Not much, but that doesn't mean he's a murderer," Gideon said. "I'd let him go home and see what happens in the next day or two, before charging him. Meanwhile you'll want the name of the neighbor who wrote that letter, and—"

Golightly ventured to interrupt. "It's all under control, Commander."

"Good," grunted Gideon.

That evening Eric Greenwood bought a later edition of the *Evening Globe*, found the story of his murder on an inside page, and read:

> Mr. Geoffrey Entwhistle, the dead woman's husband, was at Scotland Yard for several hours this afternoon, helping the police in their inquiries.

"That means they suspect him!" Greenwood muttered, and the expression in his eyes was not far short of exultation.

Entwhistle, alone in that house of evil memory, read the same paragraph, recalled the interrogation vividly, and gave a sudden, uncontrollable shiver.

Sally Dalby shivered, too. She was just coming round from a long, long sleep in that room of a thousand photographs, and she did not yet feel the horror, the shame, nor even the first onset of the longing for whatever had given her that glow of exhilaration.

The office day was over for Gideon and he felt the usual mixture of satisfaction with work done, dissatisfaction with all that had been left undone, and a slight gloom because there were matters he was a long way from being happy about. The Entwhistle murder, for one; he had not taken to the suspected man but that didn't make him a murderer, and he wondered whether anyone burdened with a sense of guilt could talk so carelessly. He hoped Golightly's efforts with the dead woman's photographs would soon bring results; if there had been a lover, he wanted to check the man's movements closely and talk to him before any arrest was made. There was obviously a possibility that Entwhistle, if scared, would do something silly; that would go a long way toward removing any doubts about him.

The nude photographs and the drug murder possibility were an even greater worry; because of his own daughters he was always sensitive to danger involving young girls. Almost guiltily, he realized that he hadn't given Penelope more than an occasional thought during the day.

There was another thing, which made Gideon angry with himself. He hadn't yet briefed Lemaitre about the church and cathedral problem. But surely there couldn't be any urgency about that.

CHAPTER 9
THE VANDAL

London's crime lay hidden under a mask of peace and quietude. The church of St. Denys, tucked away in Kensington behind the great museums, stood dark and still—except in the Lady Chapel, where a single dim bulb glowed. The South Door stood open as it always had, for the Vicar of St. Denys believed that souls could be saved at any hour of the day or night and that the best place for saving them was the church. There were many like him, but few had earned his reputation, gained in two world wars and since consolidated. In some ways he was regarded as a Fighting Parson, although nowadays there were few who could more truly be called men of peace.

His vicarage was a street away, for St. Denys was sandwiched between two massive blocks of offices, built on sites cleared by bombing. No one lived next to the church except the caretakers.

The South Door led from a dark, narrow lane between the church and one of the dimly lit office buildings. A man appeared from the direction of a car park near the Albert Hall, walking on rubber-soled shoes. His advance was not furtive, nor could it be called bold. He glanced over his shoulder as he neared the church, clearly visible had anyone been there to see, noticed no one, and turned into the lane.

A moment or two later, he pushed wider the South Door and stepped inside. He did not hesitate but stepped straight to the altar, which apparently he knew well. He went behind it, a shadowy figure, pale-faced, a man of medium build and height. He knelt down. At first it looked as if he were praying with his back to the cross, but in fact his hands were busy. He took out an object that looked like a candle with a very long wick and pushed this beneath the altar, tucking it close against the marble. He withdrew, bent down on one knee, took a lighter from his pocket and snapped it on.

Flame flickered.

He picked up the end of the fuse, held the flame to it, and kept his hand steady as the strands slowly caught. He carried the fuse, the flame gaining rapidly in strength, close to the steps leading to the nave, put it down, and without a backward glance walked out of the South Door. Outside in the alley he waited only long enough to see if anyone was in the street, then walked briskly toward the car park. He was near it when he heard a muffled explosion. It had no outward effect on him, and he stepped into a pale blue Morris 1000, one of the most commonplace cars in England, and drove off.

His thin, austere face was quite relaxed. It showed no sign of vindication or rejoicing, of pleasure or of gloating; only the rather arid satisfaction of a man whose task is done.

Several people heard the explosion, one of them a young policeman in Princes Way, one a taxi driver waiting for a fare to come out of a block of flats near the Albert Hall, one a young woman at a window on the third floor of a house nearly opposite the car park—the only house within sight of the church. She was restless and, for no particular reason, walked to the window. She saw the man, heard the explosion, heard a car engine start up and, a few minutes afterward, saw a shabby Morris appear from the car park and nose its way along the street.

The policeman was very alert.

In his experience an explosion was followed up by some kind of flurry. If a gas or an oil heater had burst, as they sometimes did, the alarm was quickly raised; but he saw and heard no one, although he was quite sure it had been no small matter.

The thing which sprang to his mind immediately was: someone's blown a safe. No one would create a flurry after that.

Should he call for help? Or should he first find out what had happened? If he brought a patrol car for nothing he would look a proper fool; on the other hand if he didn't and a burglary was reported next morning, he would never forgive himself. He quickened his pace, sure of the direction from which the sound of the explosion had come. One of the two big office blocks, most likely—there must be dozens of safes in each of them.

All was still and silent.

Across the road was a telephone kiosk, and making a swift decision he went into it and dialed 999.

"Wait there," the Information Room Inspector ordered.

Less than two minutes later, a car pulled up at the corner, and the police constable recognized men from his own Division. The driver leaned out.

"What's on, Charley?"

"I heard a bang."

"Getting nervous out here on your own?"

"No, seriously. It came from along here." The constable looked toward St. Denys, without giving the church a thought. "Might have been in one of the offices."

"We'll find out," the driver said. "See anyone?"

"I heard a car, that's all. It must have gone the other way."

"Let's check," said the man next to the driver. They climbed out of the car, three big, matter-of-fact detectives whose job was simply to seek out bad men, and walked with long strides toward the buildings—and incidentally toward St. Denys. As they passed the end of the lane the uniformed man saw a flicker of raw, undisciplined light.

"Look!" he exclaimed.

"The church!" breathed the driver. "Come on!"

They turned hurriedly into the lane, and as they neared the door flames showed vividly at a small window. One man spun round, ejaculating "Fire!" and ran back to the car. The others thrust their way into the church, and as they did so the red and yellow of leaping flames shone on their faces, on the pillars, on the choir stalls. Regimental standards, hanging in tatters, were already alight, a magnificent seventeenth-century tapestry was smoldering, the altar cloth and the rich Persian runner in front of and behind the altar were in flames. The altar itself had been smashed to smithereens, and pieces of marble had been flung about the nave, striking walls and wood but, strangely, missing the windows.

The three policemen tore at the standards, then the tapestry, stamping out what they could, until the fire brigade bell sounded and a fire engine roared up.

Gideon did not hear about the latest sacrilegious vandalism until half-past eight next morning, when he was about to leave for the office. Kate was in the kitchen, looking through a daily newspaper; all the children were out, including Penelope, who had appeared quite bright and cheerful. Gideon answered the telephone, which was in the hall of this high-ceilinged Victorian house, and leaned against the side of the staircase as he did so.

"George?" It was Hobbs.

"Hallo."

"Are you on your way?"

"Nearly."

"Good," said Hobbs. "I've put my foot in it."

"What's 'it'?" asked Gideon, covering his surprise at such an admission.

"I thought you'd told Lemaitre about the church investigation, but he doesn't seem to know anything about it."

"My fault," said Gideon promptly. He felt sure this wasn't the sole reason for the call. "I was pushed for time and wanted to brief him properly. What brought the question up?"

"There was an explosion in St. Denys Church, Kensington, last night," answered Hobbs. "I found Lemaitre here and asked him why he wasn't at Kensington. The remark wasn't appreciated."

"I can imagine," Gideon said. It was a thousand pities that Hobbs *had* got off on the wrong foot with Lemaitre, but that wasn't the pre-eminent worry: the church affair was. "Where's Lemaitre now?" he asked.

"Here. Says he'll go to St. Denys on your instructions or not at all."

There was, as always, something reserved about Hobbs, and it would be easy to infer a kind of criticism—that he, Gideon, should not have allowed this situation to develop. Gideon pushed the thought aside.

"Have me transferred to him," he said. "And I'll be late. I'll go to St. Denys first."

"Very well," said Hobbs.

Lemaitre was soon on the line.

"Lemaitre," he announced with an excessive precision which indicated that he was standing on his dignity.

"Meet me at St. Denys as soon as you can get there," Gideon ordered. "Bring a driver, and look through the papers the Dean brought me yesterday while you're on your way."

"Er—" said Lemaitre, his tone softening; and then it hardened again. "Right!"

Twenty minutes later, Gideon drew up near the church and saw Lemaitre getting out of a car a hundred yards away. A police car and a builder's van were parked nearby, and there was a small crowd of people, mostly young, two policemen and several newspaper reporters and photographers. One of the reporters came up to Gideon, a sandy-haired man whose round face was peppered with freckles.

"Taking this seriously then, Commander?" He had a faint Scottish accent.

"We always take crime seriously," Gideon replied gravely.

Another, older, hard-faced man spoke, and two cameras clicked, one flashing bright against the dark buildings and an overcast sky.

"Do you think there is a campaign against the Church, Mr. Gideon?"

Gideon's reaction was swift as light, but he did not make the mistake of answering too quickly.

"Good Lord, no! What makes you ask such a question?"

"There was a break-in at St. Ludd's Cathedral, remember."

"There have been thefts from churches since there were churches," Gideon said dryly. "Gold and silver still have a good value whether they come from a private house, a museum, or a church." He looked up at Lemaitre, who had a way of walking which seemed to use up a lot of energy, knees slightly knocking, arms swinging with unnecessary vigor. He was smiling his official smile.

"Good morning, Commander."

"Good morning, Superintendent."

"Commander," the sandy-haired man asked, "is it true that Chief Superintendent Hobbs is to be the next Deputy Commander?"

All the Press men were looking at Lemaitre, not at Gideon, and Gideon half feared a sharp reaction from Lemaitre. Instead, his grin broadened and he said bluffly, "Couldn't be a better man if he is."

"Can I quote you?" the hard-faced man asked.

"There's nothing to quote," Gideon said. "No appointment's been made. You *can* quote me as saying that we'd be glad to hear from anyone who knows about the trouble here last night—if any man or woman was seen, on foot or in a car, if anything was heard—the usual things. That way, you'll be helping us." He moved toward the lane, and Lemaitre followed. A policeman moved aside, nodding, inarticulate. Two or three big pieces of marble stood outside the South Door, another policeman by them. "Lem," Gideon said, "it looks as if there's something very ugly brewing, and this may be part of it. It was on my agenda for this morning."

"I know," Lemaitre said, grinning broadly. "You'd made a note and clipped it to the envelope the Dean left. I took it home to read, because you'd put 'Lem to read' on it." He was very pleased with himself, with reason, and Gideon repressed an obvious query: why had he put on an act with Hobbs?

"Then you know more about the trouble than I do," Gideon said. "We won't talk about it here, but does this crime fit the pattern?"

"Haven't seen any pattern yet."

"It's what we're looking for." Gideon stepped inside the church, the door of which was blocked open.

The first glimpse was enough to appall both Yard men. In the daylight that filtered through one stained glass and four plain glass windows, the damage was shown up vividly. Pieces of marble had been violently hurled about, cracking pews, seriously damaging some beautifully painted heraldry on the choir stalls. The lectern, with its magnificent brass eagle, had been smashed, a dozen oil paintings had been ruined, the old medieval font had a big piece out of it. The aisles were littered with debris. At the wall near the altar were the charred remains of the standards, and the blackened end of the big tapestry showed how nearly that, too, had been destroyed. Of the altar itself only a few broken pieces remained in position.

On his knees a Fire Service officer, whom Gideon knew slightly as an expert in arson, was minutely examining the heart of the explosion. Police photographers from the Division, as well as detectives from Fingerprints, were going about their jobs with a disciplined application that Gideon liked to see.

Watching them all was the Reverend Miles Chaplin.

He was a man whom Gideon had met when taking part in the British Legion March Past at the Cenotaph, and on other occasions when the Church and the Army shared some ceremonial or memorial service. Almost completely bald, he was a remarkable man to look at.

His cheeks were lean, his nose finely curved, while his hooded eyes, deeply sunken beneath a wide forehead, held the sharp alertness of a predatory bird. He stood in his black cassock, arms folded across his chest; it was impossible even to guess what he was thinking.

Gideon went up to him. "I couldn't be more sorry, Vicar."

Chaplin glanced at him without recognition, and replied in a clipped, high-pitched voice, "Nor could I."

"I am Commander Gideon of Scotland Yard," Gideon said, and received a brief glance of interest. "This is Chief Superintendent Lemaitre."

"Lemaitre!" Chaplin said sharply, his interest now fully aroused. He stared into Lemaitre's equally bony but far less arresting face.

"Morning, padre," Lemaitre said, in the tone of an old familiar, if not a friend.

CHAPTER 10
OLD FRIENDS

Gideon saw the real pleasure in the Vicar's eyes, matching the glow in Lemaitre's. The two men gripped hands for what seemed a long time, as if this were a true reunion. No one else seemed to notice. Their hands dropped as Lemaitre said, "Bloody bad business this—Sorry, padre! I forgot where I was. Any idea who did it?"

"I most certainly have not."

"We've got to find the basket," Lemaitre said. "Any hate campaign, threats or that kind of thing?"

"None whatsoever," said Chaplin. "Except of course, that this is a declaration of hate in itself. It is a very terrible thing, a shocking thing." The eyes were very bright beneath those heavy lids. "Do you believe in evil, Commander?"

Gideon answered, "In a way."

"Don't you think this is an evil act?"

"Yes."

"Carried out by an evil man?"

"Or a sick one," Gideon said.

"Please, please," protested Chaplin in a sharp voice. "I hardly expect a senior officer of Scotland Yard to pay even lip service to this modern psychiatric jargon. Evil is evil, sin is sin, a man possessed of the devil is not sick. It may be possible—it *is* possible, to my certain knowledge—to cast the devil out, but it is not sickness."

"I know exactly how you feel, sir," Gideon said. "You must forgive me if I see this simply as a crime committed—it is no part of my job to say why it was done, only who did it. Is this the first act of vandalism carried out here?"

"*Vandalism?* Sacrilege, you mean."

"Is it the first crime?" demanded Gideon. He was troubled by the old man's manner and disappointed, because his reputation was that of a tolerant and broad-minded cleric. Had he changed? Or had the attack so angered him that it had temporarily blocked a cooler judgment?

"No," said Chaplin. "It is not the first crime in this house of God. There have been others. Three times in the past few weeks the offertory boxes have been broken open and the contents stolen. Hymn books and books of Common Prayer are often despoiled by tearing, or by offensive words scribbled across the pages. It is an outrage I find it hard, even impossible, to forgive."

"Have you reported this to the police?"

"The thefts, yes. It seems quite beyond your capacity to prevent such crimes, which are now commonplace throughout London. There was a day when an offertory box was considered sacred, when a church was truly a sanctuary. The attitude in this so-called civilized age is quite different. There is no respect for the law, none for the church."

At these impassioned words everyone looked at the old man, whose voice was rising steadily to a crescendo of denunciation. Anger flashed from his eyes as if he were preaching a sermon which would soon lead to a general threat of hell-fire and damnation.

Abruptly, he stopped.

A girl of about eighteen had entered. She looked young and fresh and quite purposeful in this scene of destruction and defeat as she came forward. Every eye turned toward her. Chaplin seemed to draw within himself as if, the words now said, he was prepared to don again a mask of humility and forgiveness.

"I've just heard what a beastly thing has happened," she murmured, going up to him. "I *am* sorry. Mummy would have come herself, but she was not feeling up to it. Are you all right, Grandfather? It must have been a dreadful shock."

She spoke as if she were humoring a child.

"I'm perfectly all right, Elspeth," Chaplin said testily. "Why shouldn't I be?" He drew a deep breath, and went on. "But I am a little tired. If you will excuse me, gentlemen, I will go along to the Vicarage. You will find me there if you need any more information." Head high, he led the way, with the girl a step behind him.

Gideon entered his office just before eleven o'clock that morning, two hours later than usual. A detective inspector was stand-in for Lemaitre, and it was immediately evident that Lemaitre had been away: the reports were in the wrong order, explanatory notes were much more prolix, Gideon had a feeling that things could misfire. Instead, it was he who was wrong. The internal telephone rang five minutes after he arrived; it was Hobbs.

"How did things go?"

"There won't be anything to worry about with Lem," Gideon answered. "Humor him a bit, that's all."

"I'll try," Hobbs said quietly. "Was there much damage?"

"Far too much," said Gideon. "I want to settle down for an hour with the Dean's papers as soon as I can. Have you seen anyone?"

"Yes. Rollo, with nothing to report. Golightly says he hasn't had any response at all to his photograph inquiry. We've turned the St. Ludd's burglar over to the City Police, he's up for a hearing any time now. Simmons wants another week before he can brief us thoroughly on that Hobjoy fraud case, and won't commit himself beyond that. There's nothing much in this morning—the usual crop from burglary to breaking and entering, shoplifting to bag-snatching. Two men raided a post office out at Eltham but were scared off by a dog who tore a patch out of a pair of trousers. Seventeen cars were stolen in the Metropolitan area last night. West Central raided a strip club which provided cubicles for the members to have private shows. The manager and two of the strippers will be up this morning for running a disorderly house—"

"Are they known?" Gideon interrupted.

"Guy Mason's the manager."

"Oh, that mob," Gideon said. "Close 'em down in one place and they bob up in another. Yes?"

"A hit and run in Brompton Road, Knightsbridge," Hobbs went on in his precise way. "A light-gray Jaguar was involved. Alleged rape on Wimbledon Common, a truckload of cigarettes stolen from the Goods Yard at Paddington. The Newcastle police are worried about the death of the man found sitting in his car, they think it was murder—can we send someone to check on some rather suspicious details? Brighton aren't happy about that child's body found in the sea and they're asking for information from other seaside resorts. The lungs contained sea water all right, but also some particles of seaweed not commonly found in the Channel."

"What did you do?" interrupted Gideon.

"I recommended getting a few specimens and the autopsy report and sending them round to other resorts," Hobbs said.

"Do that, will you?"

"Yes. Apart from all this, nothing," Hobbs added.

Gideon said "Good," and ran off without considering the irony of Hobbs's final words. *Good.* It was a catalogue of crimes of nearly every conceivable variety, and yet it posed no new major problems. The important ones remained the Entwhistle murder, the nude photographs case, and the church crimes. Although he still felt a sense of disquiet about the murdered girls and the missing photographer, he did not dwell on it but sat at his desk to study the report that Dean

Howcroft had brought and which Lemaitre had read ahead of
time. Hobbs's recital, so lucid and comprehensive, left him
with a feeling of satisfaction that the new Deputy Commander to be was the right man.

Soon he was absorbed in the Dean's report, which covered
incidents in the Southern and Home Counties.

He began to feel worried, for the second page showed that
the total number of "offenses" in the past twelve months was
over a thousand, only a few of which had been reported to
the police. The major items on the list were:

Damage to hymn and prayer books	—107 instances affecting 2,501 books
Damage to fonts	—18
Defilement of fonts	—18
Damage to altar and dossal cloths	—142
Slashing of vestments	—41
Damage to missals	—375
Forced and rifled alms boxes	—36
Damage to heat and light systems	—48
Damage to stained-glass windows	—40

Each one in itself was hardly a serious crime, and it was
understandable that the church authorities, aware of the current attitude of almost morbid tolerance toward criminals,
should be nervous of risking an indignant outcry at so-called
unchristian behavior if they appealed to the police; it wasn't
surprising that they had taken action so tardily.

A cautious note in the memorandum followed:

The nature of these instances gives some reason to suspect
willful and malicious damage by a church member or other
person associated with the church, but the number and fre-
quency of the offenses now make it appear possible that the
offenses were caused by outside interference. As so many of
the offenses were similar it seems possible that the perpetrators were in collusion. No Baptist or Quaker premises
have been affected, and very few Congregationalist or Methodist.

Gideon thought: Why oh why didn't they come to us earlier?

Almost at that very moment, a young commercial photographer named Henry Rhodes was entering the cellar in which

Sally Dalby had been photographed and was saying to himself, *Why the hell didn't I come here earlier?* He was frightened because he knew that the police wanted to interview him and he was fairly certain that once they questioned him it would lead to his arrest. For one thing, he had sold a great number of those "artistic" photographs to customers at the shops; for another, he had employed a number of agents to sell them to workers in big stores, offices, and factories. There was little doubt that he would be charged and found guilty under one section or another of the Obscene Publications Act, resulting in a sentence of at least six months' imprisonment. Since a friend at the chemist's shop where he worked had tipped him off about a police inquiry, he had been in hiding with a girl friend who had been happy to share her bed and board without asking questions.

But he was nearly broke and needed money. This cellar in Tottenham was the obvious place to come, for Toni Bottelli worked here, and Toni was close to Mr. Big, if he wasn't Mr. Big himself.

Rhodes, until two years ago an unworldly young man from a small provincial city in the Midlands, felt excitement stirring at the thought of "Mr. Big." There was great drama in it for him, as there had been drama and excitement at being on the fringe of crime. He had drifted into it, selling a few nasty pictures for a joke among friends, and had been paid well for running off a few prints in the darkroom at the shop. Now, eighteen months afterward, he earned over £2000 a year from this "spare-time" occupation—and spent up to the hilt, on girls, on the dogs, and on casino gambling. He had always been fond of showing off and had always been a success with "the ladies." He had a natural, easy manner, and he was a curiously forthright individual, who would tell a girl that he liked her legs, her face or her bosom without thinking there was anything overbold in it. That was the way they were made, wasn't it? Consequently, he had fallen naturally into this job. Persuading girls to pose had seldom been difficult; nor had selling the pictures. He saw no harm in either, and would hold forth indignantly if challenged.

"All the great artists paint nudes, don't they?" "Take all the nudes off a museum wall and you wouldn't have much left, would you?" "And what about statues? Haven't you ever heard of Michelangelo? Look at some of his, men *and* women. *He* didn't hide much." "Lot of prudes, that's what people are."

This, then, was his honest conviction.

Now he went through the small tobacconist's shop above

the cellar where Toni Bottelli worked. An elderly woman in the shop, a *madame* to the girls who came here, knew him and allowed him through. The cellar was approached by a concealed door in the wall of a staircase, Bottelli knowing very well that a police raid could be very awkward.

Rhodes pressed a warning bell, slid the door open, and went downstairs. As he stepped into the cellar he heard a flurry of movement, saw Bottelli throw a toweling robe over a girl on the cushions on the dais.

"Okay, okay, I'm used to it," Rhodes sang out.

Bottelli stood with his back to the girl, glaring. "What the hell do you want?"

"Just a little bit of lolly, Toni."

"Who told you to come here?"

"I told myself," said Rhodes, jauntily.

"Well, get to hell out of it and don't come back unless I send for you!"

Rhodes caught his breath. "Now take it easy," he protested. "That's no way to talk."

"It's the way I'm talking to you! Get the hell out of it!"

Rhodes spoke more angrily. "Don't you talk to me like that."

"Get out, or I'll throw you out!"

"Oh, will you," Rhodes said. Inwardly he was feeling scared, but nothing in his voice or manner showed it. "I'd like to see you try."

They stood facing each other, Rhodes appalled, Bottelli viciously angry. Gradually, Rhodes's anger began to fade into anxiety. He needed help and needed somewhere to hide, and this man had introduced him to the business. There was no one else to go to.

"Get *out*," Bottelli growled.

"Listen, Toni, you don't understand—"

"I don't have to understand. *You* have to."

"Toni, I need some money! I'm on the run!"

The last words came out as Bottelli began to move forward, his hands outstretched, his eyes shimmering with anger. At first, the phrase "I'm on the run" had no effect, but suddenly he stopped short, caught his breath, and ejaculated, "You're *what?*"

"I'm on the run. The cops are after me! You always said you'd see me right if I ran into trouble. How about proving it?"

As he spoke, Rhodes stared at the handsome man in front of him, wondering what lay behind the inscrutability of his eyes. Nothing in them gave Rhodes the slightest inkling of the truth.

"If the cops catch him," Bottelli was thinking, "he'll talk. And he's not going to talk." Without consciously putting it in so many words, his mind went smoothly on: "I wonder which way I'd better get rid of him."

CHAPTER 11
ONCE A KILLER

Henry Rhodes's lips and mouth felt dry as he stared at Bottelli, who had hardly moved since hearing the other say, "I'm on the run." The girl on the couch didn't stir, but he was not concerned with her; had he given her a thought he would have assumed that she was lying doggo. Bottelli's eyes began to narrow, and suddenly he smiled, showing his vivid white teeth.

Rhodes's heart leapt with relief.

"So you're on the run," Bottelli said. "How come, Henry?"

"The cops got hold of some of the pictures, some blabbermouth at the Bowling Lanes told them where he'd got them from."

"When did this happen?"

"Monday."

"Monday! God! It's Thursday now."

"I've been lying low."

Bottelli said very softly, "So you've been lying low, have you? Where?"

"Katey Lyle's place."

"You've been laying while you've been lying low, have you? She's quite a doll."

"She's a doll all right."

"But you let her go."

"I ran out of the lolly, Toni."

"So you ran out on the cops and you ran out of the dough and after that you ran out on Katey Lyle."

"You make it sound like I was always running out," Rhodes protested peevishly. "I thought I was doing the right thing."

"And so you were, Henry," Bottelli said. "You've got to keep away from the cops and there's only one way of doing that—get out of the country until they cool off you."

Rhodes's eyes lit up. "Then that's what I'll do!"

"You'll certainly need some lolly," Bottelli said. "And a plane ride—how about luggage and things?"

"I've got some over at Katey's." Rhodes could hardly conceal his pleasure.

"That's fine," said Bottelli. "Now I know a man who can fix you a cheap flight to France—you got a passport?"

"Why, sure!"

"At Katey's?"

"That's right."

"You thought of everything, didn't you," Bottelli said smoothly. "Okay, Henry. You go back to Katey's and stay there until after dark. I'll arrange for a Honda motorcycle to be parked outside her place, and I'll drop an ignition key through the letter box, with directions as to the place to go. It will be in a field near Ashford, Kent, or near Southend—I'm not sure yet. You'll find the two-seater plane and a pilot waiting for you, and you'll be dropped in France with the motorbike and some dough. Right?"

"It sounds wonderful!" Rhodes's voice was high-pitched. "I knew you'd see me through, Toni. I can't tell you how grateful I am."

"Think nothing of it," Toni Bottelli said.

As far as Henry Rhodes could judge, everything went according to plan, and fair-haired, plump-bodied Katey Lyle could not have been sweeter nor more compliant. He rode to Southend with directions in his pocket, helmet on his head, wind whistling past his goggles, happy as a young man could be. Even when he turned into the field, indicated by a white circle on the bark of a tree close to the gate, and found no sign of an aircraft, he was unperturbed; it had been delayed, that was all.

He waited by the gate, on a bright starlit evening.

He heard a rustling, but did not suspect danger. He had not the slightest sense of impending death, and in fact was whistling softly, looking up into the sky for the aircraft which was never to come.

He felt a sudden, sharp, bruising blow between his shoulder blades, heard the muffled roar of a shot—and died.

He was Toni Bottelli's fourth victim, and the first one whom Bottelli had murdered by shooting.

Soon the murderer was heading back on the Honda for

London and for Sally Dalby, who was probably still asleep on the dais in the cellar of photographs.

About the time that Henry Rhodes died, Gideon was sitting at the table in the kitchen at his home, watching amateur boxing on a small television set. The volume was turned low and he listened with half an ear to the cascade of the piano as Penelope played in the living room. The rest of the family was out. Penelope went on playing with a fury of abandon which gradually pierced Gideon's consciousness and he got up slowly and went to her. She was playing the Grieg Concerto, and he had never known her to play with such fire and such virtuosity; even he, the unmusical member of the family, was impressed and admiring. He stepped just inside the room. The piano, a Bechstein grand bought years ago when the Gideons had realized that they had two gifted daughters, was in the far corner, and Penelope's back was toward him. Her fair hair rippled down past her shoulders. Her slender body moved with the concentrated tension of the playing. Her fingers seemed to dance over the keys as if she had four hands, not two. As she reached the final crescendo her very life seemed to be part of the wonderful sound.

When she stopped she sat motionless, fingers still poised.

Gideon, remembering how dreadfully she had been disappointed only yesterday morning, wondered what was going through her mind now—would despair surge over her again? When she sprang to her feet he was taken by surprise, and had no time to back out of sight.

Her eyes were glowing, and her radiant young face lit up even more when she saw him.

"Daddy!" she cried. "I *am* good, I know I am!"

"My God, you're good!" Gideon said fervently.

"*You* could tell?"

"If that examiner were here now—"

"I know, but it was my fault, I gave it the wrong interpretation, I tried to be too clever. There *will* be another chance, and next time I'm going to play this, and I'll pass. I know I will."

"You'll pass," said Gideon. "Penny—"

"Daddy, you're wonderful!" she cried, and threw her arms about him. As he felt the strength of her young body and saw the glow in her eyes, he felt a moment of sheer exultation— that she was his daughter; his, and Kate's. She was still hugging him in her new-found delight when the telephone bell rang.

She gave him a final hug and broke away.

"I expect it will be for you."

"Probably." Gideon stepped back into the hall, lifted off the receiver and said, "George Gideon."

"George." He recognized Rollo's voice on the instant, and a pang went through him, because this was probably to do with the three dead girls. "Sorry to worry you so late, but I've got a nasty one."

"Another body?" Gideon pictured the photographs he had seen the previous afternoon and heard Penelope playing, very subdued this time, so that he could hear what was being said.

"Different sex," said Rollo. "That photographer I was looking for, Henry Rhodes. He's turned up dead. Freak chance we found him so soon. A courting couple going into a field nearly fell over the body."

"How was he killed?" Gideon demanded.

"Shot in the back."

"Where?"

"Five miles from Southend. They had his photograph—I'd sent it out—and called me. I'd like to go down there with a couple of our own chaps and get cracking under floodlights. If those three girls were killed by the same man and he's killed Rhodes to keep him quiet—sorry, George, I know I'm doing a Lemaitre on you. All right for me to go?"

Gideon said, "Yes. You don't need an official request for help from the Essex people, as we want him for the London jobs."

"Put a call in to square things for me, will you?" asked Rollo.

Gideon said, "All right." He was about to ring off when a thought flashed through his mind. "Hugh!"

"I'm still here."

"Have you been checking closely on other missing girls?"

"You bet I have."

"How many have been reported?"

"This week, six," answered Rollo. "Last week, three. Multiply by at least five and you've got the number of those who are really missing. If parents would only make sure we knew in good time. . . ." This was Rollo's hobbyhorse, which, once started, must never be allowed free rein.

"Quite, quite," interrupted Gideon soothingly, "I'm absolutely with you. But, let me see, *how* many girls did you say have the statistics we're looking for?"

"Two," answered Rollo.

"Names?"

"A Doris Manning, of Salisbury, and a Sally Dalby, who comes from Guildford. She's the latest—her father reported her missing only yesterday. Apparently she told a friend that she was going to pose in the nude for a photographer."

"Did she, by George!" Gideon's voice rose. "Get her photograph out and a general call for her."

"First thing in the morning," Rollo promised.

"Tonight," ordered Gideon, and then remembered. "You want to get down to Essex, of course. I'll see to the other thing, then."

"Why not Golightly?" suggested Rollo, with a chuckle in his voice. "He's had an easy one over the Entwhistle case and he's at the Yard now."

After a moment's pause, Gideon said, "Put me through to him, will you?"

Geoffrey Entwhistle lay back in an armchair, a whisky bottle by his side, a nearly empty glass in his hand. He wasn't drunk, but at least he was not remembering the past so vividly, not regretting so much his decision to leave home for three years. He had left because he had seen his marriage breaking up and had thought desperately that a long parting would help. He had come back believing that he could settle down to a new life.

If things went on as they were, it would be a new life all right—a life sentence in prison for a murder he hadn't committed.

The whisky created a hazy kind of resignation and the ability to face facts without alarm. Fact: he was under suspicion for the murder of Margaret, his wife. Fact: he hadn't felt any grief at her death. Fact: he had been away from his children for so long that they were strangers to him and he to them. Fact: his mother-in-law hated him, believed he had killed Margaret, and was busily making sure the children believed it, too. Fact: he had not killed Margaret.

Probability: by tomorrow he would be charged with the murder.

He gave a snort that was half laugh, half groan, gulped down the whisky in the glass, and picked up the bottle.

Eric Greenwood stood looking at the photograph of Margaret, whom he had murdered, for a long time. Slowly and deliberately he picked it up and carried it to the empty fireplace in his living room. He put the photograph in this and set light to a corner; the flame caught tardily, gradually crinkling the face and then devouring the print bit by bit. Before the last flicker, he turned to a desk, full of his private papers, and began to search through it for letters and notes which Marga-

ret had sent him. He made a pile of these in the grate and
burned them also.

Watching these higher, consuming flames and not knowing
the strange light they cast upon his eyes, he said aloud, "It's a
good thing I never wrote to her."

He had always been very careful about this, so anxious had
he been to avoid any involvement in divorce.

He did not believe in divorce.

"Percy," Gideon said, "I've an urgent job for you."

"I'll buy it," Percy Golightly said.

"A girl named Sally Dalby is reported missing. I want
her photograph and description sent out on a general call.
Tonight."

"Don't remind me of photographs," Golightly protested.
"There hasn't been a single bite about Margaret Entwhistle's."

"How is that shaping?"

"Looks more and more like the husband," answered Golightly. "The mother-in-law let her hair down tonight. According to her the Entwhistles used to quarrel like hell before
he left for Thailand. She was too flighty for his liking. Looks
more and more as if he came back, goaded by that anonymous letter, and let his wife have it."

"We'll talk about that in the morning," Gideon said. "Fix
the call for Sally Dalby."

There was something about the name that attracted him:
Sally Dalby. He was sensitive about young women tonight, of
course, but that kind of oversensitiveness did no harm. He
tried to put all the Yard's cases out of mind and picked up the
newspaper, but inside ten minutes he was reading the *Police
Gazette*. It was late before he heard a key in the front door
and got up to greet Kate, who was bright-eyed and tired
after a visit to the cinema with a neighbor.

"Oh, put that thing away, George!" She flicked a hand
toward the *Police Gazette*. "You should have come with me
tonight, you would have enjoyed it almost as much as if it had
been a Western. Some of that South African country is beautiful and the photography was absolutely breathtaking. . . ."

Drinking tea and eating biscuits, listening to Kate's enthusi-
astic chatter, seeing the children as they came home one after
the other, four of them living at home these days, Gideon forgot all the problems of the Yard. It was when he was in bed,
Kate by his side, that he thought: I hope there's no more
trouble in the churches tonight.

CHAPTER 12
FOUR-IN-ONE

Police Constable Edmund Davies was a man in his middle thirties, keen on his job but unambitious, a contented family man who took it for granted that one day he would be promoted to sergeant, that he would retire at fifty-five and take on a part-time job. He had one hobby, gardening; one sport, boxing. It was two years since he had last been to church—at the christening of his third born.

Like every other policeman in the London area, he was on the *qui vive* that night whenever he neared one of the three churches on his beat. There had been a special instructions during the day that every church should be watched, door handles tried, vergers and clergymen, where possible, asked what precautions were normally taken. This was a routine commonly applied to cinemas, theaters, banks and post offices, but it was new and comparatively exciting where churches were concerned.

Davies' favorite church was St. Ethelreda's.

He liked the weathered gray stone and the smooth, beautifully kept grass, and the hill it was on. Once it had overlooked farm and meadow land; now masses of red roofs and chimney pots, ribbon roads, and factories, clustering the reservoir, lay beneath it. In this part of the outskirts of London, the countryside which Davies loved was still within easy distance, and he liked to stand by day near the church gate and look northwest. One, in the myriad mass of houses, was his own; one of the little green patches was the one where he labored so lovingly.

Tonight there was a slight drizzle, misting the lights in windows and creating halos about the bright street lamps. Over the doorway of the church was a single electric lamp in a wire shade, for the vicar of St. Ethelreda's liked the church to be available for prayer by night as well as day.

Davies plodded up the hill. A car passed, wheels slithering on the damp macadam. A cyclist wobbled by; two couples passed on the other side of the road, oblivious of the rain. The misted light glowing outside the church porch burned steadily.

"No one would ever do anything there," Davies thought, but the reflection did not make him careless. He opened the gate, noted its creak, and walked slowly up the tarred path. Only the sounds of night were about him, and he was so used to this lonely job that he did not give a moment's thought to danger.

He put a hand on the wrought-iron latch and pushed the door open.

As he did so a dark figure leaped out of the faint yellow light that filled the church. Taken completely by surprise, Davies had no time to protect himself. The man launched his body forward and an out-flung foot caught Davies in the groin. Agony shot through him as he staggered to one side.

His assailant dashed through the door and was lost to sight.

Davies was so pain-racked that for seconds he almost forgot where he was. Flung up against the wall, he saved himself from falling, then bent down, jackknifing his body to stave off the worst of the pain.

He was aware of the flickering, spitting light, but not yet of its significance. He forced his head between his knees until gradually the waves of pain eased. Slowly he became increasingly conscious of the unusual quality of the light. Straightening up, he saw a tiny spot of bright flame on the floor at the far end of the nave, and a word ripped into his head.

"Dynamite!"

Fighting waves of pain and of fear, he staggered toward the altar, understanding at last exactly what was causing the spitting and spluttering: a lighted fuse. He must put it out. Once he fell against the end of a pew, the jarring blow bringing on a wave of excruciating pain. It held him back for precious seconds, but he was driven by the desperate urgency of the situation: he *must* put that fuse out.

Not once did the thought of personal danger occur to him.

He actually managed to quicken his pace, until he saw the flame close to the side of the altar and sensed that there was little time. The fire was now spitting more wildly, and he scrambled down on his hands and knees, able to see the two sticks of dynamite to which the fuse was attached. There was only an inch unburned. He had nothing with which to dowse the flame and unhesitatingly thrust his hand forward, to press his palm onto it.

There was a sudden, blinding flash, a roar, and awful pain in his eyes and in his right hand; then he lost consciousness.

In the churchyard were two lovers, sheltered beneath a yew tree, dry and secure and satisfied, lying close but still as they looked into each other's eyes. Suddenly a flash lit up the entire scene. There was a roar and the sound of crashing glass. The man started up, and a sliver of glass stabbed into his cheek.

"God!" he gasped.

"Jock!" cried the girl. "What is it?"

"It's in the church." He leaped up. "Go and telephone the police. Go on, hurry!" When she bent down, scrambling for her shoes, he screamed again, "Hurry! Hurry!"

Sobbing, bewildered, she moved uncertainly away as he ran toward the front of the church, oblivious of a dribble of blood splashing down his cheek.

In northeast London; near Charlton in South London; in Camberwell; and in southwest London, close to Putney Bridge, other churches suffered the same kind of damage, but no one was hurt.

Gideon woke to a morning of bright sunshine and was cheerful because of it. Kate was still sleeping, and he left her undisturbed. Creeping downstairs, he made some tea and toast, and was out of the house by seven-forty-five. He kept his car garaged round the corner and was nearly out of earshot of the house when his telephone began to ring; he went back, muttering.

It was Lamaitre.

"Okay, I'll see him at the office," Gideon said.

The Embankment road was clear and Gideon was at the Yard in twenty minutes. He saw Lemaitre's car; Lem was really making sure he kept on top of this job. A constable fresh on duty saluted Gideon but no one else was about. He opened the door of his office and, as it closed, Lemaitre's door opened. Lemaitre's eyes had the glassy look which follows a sleepless night; he hadn't shaved, his collar and bow tie had a crumpled look.

Gideon's heart dropped. "More?"

"Four more."

"Why didn't you call me?"

"You've got enough on your plate."

Gideon let that pass. "Where did they happen?"

"Different parts of London. There's worse."

"What?"

"One of our chaps had a hand blown off, and was blinded. He was trying to stop the explosion."

Quite suddenly, Gideon went cold. Few things were more precious to him than the security and safety of his men, and this news came so unexpectedly that it hurt badly. It was several seconds before he asked, "Where did that happen?"

"St. Ethelreda's, Wimbley."

"On the hill?"

"Yes."

"When?"

"About eleven o'clock."

Just after Kate had come in, Gideon remembered.

"A couple canoodling in the churchyard heard it, and sent for our chaps. They found Davies—"

"The injured constable?"

"Yes. Got him into hospital within twenty minutes."

"Isn't there any doubt about the injury to his eyes?"

Lemaitre answered wearily, "No, George." He sat down on the arm of a chair opposite the desk. "I've just come from the hospital. Saw his wife there—plucky woman. I promised her we'd see she's all right."

"All right," Gideon echoed bitterly.

"You know what I mean."

"Sure you do. Anything to help us find who did it?"

"Nothing to help with any one of the four," Lemaitre said. "George, I could do with a cuppa."

"Sorry," Gideon said. He lifted a telephone. "Tea, in a pot, and some breakfast for Mr. Lemaitre. Make it snappy." He rang off before there was time for an answer and picked up a box of cigarettes kept for visitors. Lemaitre took one, and lit up. "Four separate crimes. Timing?"

"Two were undoutedly short-time fuses, as in all probability were the others. The explosions were all within ten or fifteen minutes of eleven o'clock, so we must assume there were four different men." When Gideon hesitated, Lemaitre drew deeply on the cigarette and said, "Okay, okay, or women."

"None of them seen?"

"A car was heard to start off after each explosion, but that doesn't mean much," Lemaitre said. "No one's come forward to say they saw prowlers about. There's one thing, though. We found a girl who saw a man walk away from St. Denys the night before last. He was a small fellow wearing a bowler hat and carrying an umbrella. She thinks he drove off in a pale-colored Morris 1000. A pale-colored Morris 1000 was seen parked in St. Ethelreda's Road last night. I'm following that up."

Gideon said heavily, "*Four* different churches at the same time. Lem, what have we struck? I hope to God—" He broke off.

Lemaitre frowned. "Now what?"

"Was it a mistake for me to go to St. Denys yesterday morning?"

"When it was on your route to the Yard? Been damned fishy if you hadn't."

Gideon said, "Something seems to have quickened the pace and worsened the nature of the crimes." Frowning, concentrating, he was irritated when Lemaitre grinned.

"Jumping to conclusions, aren't you?" Lemaitre quipped.

"*What?*"

"How do you know this is the same series of crimes? Could be imitative—these are much worse than any of the crimes on the Dean's list."

Gideon stared, then began to smile.

"You win," he said. "We need to check a lot of things." Before he could go on, the door opened and an elderly messenger brought in Lemaitre's breakfast and an extra cup. Gideon motioned to a table beneath one wall and the messenger put the tray down. "Tuck in," Gideon said, feeling hungry at the sight of bacon and eggs, sausages and fried bread. He poured himself a cup of tea and went to his own chair. "Morris 1000, and a man in a bowler hat carrying an umbrella. There must be thousands of the first and tens of thousands of the second. We need—" He broke off. "What do you recommend, Lem?"

"Double watch on all churches tonight," Lemaitre said. "Can't keep anything quiet any longer. If the Dean had come to us weeks ago, we might have stopped this kind of nonsense. As it is we must keep a special look out for light-colored Morrises, a check on every man who goes in or out of a church after dark tonight, and make an examination of the residual ash of the dynamite and of the container. As a matter of fact that was made by Hecht and Hecht, of Watford."

Gideon said, "Sure?"

"Certainly I'm sure. Quarry and demolition blasting dynamite, available quite freely. They've got several hundred customers in the London and the Home Counties, *and* a couple of dozen wholesalers."

"We want every dealer checked."

"I started that last night," Lemaitre mumbled through a mouthful of food.

Gideon said, "Good. Had any sleep at all?"

"Nope."

"Get home as soon as you can."

Lemaitre said, "I hope that's not an order, Commander. I want to be busy this morning."

Gideon smiled at him faintly, and said at last, "Not an order, Lem."

"Ta," said Lemaitre, and after a pause he went on. "How's Mr. Acting New Deputy Commander Mr. Basket Alec Bloody Hobbs getting on?"

"I'll find out when he comes in."

"He's been in for an hour," said Lemaitre. "Your henchmen really work these days, George. *You* can take it easy."

Gideon didn't answer but thought bleakly that he did not see any likelihood of taking anything easy until the church crimes were solved. If five men had been involved, why not fifteen? Or fifty? That seemed to him the most significant question, and against it, all other investigations seemed negligible, for there was no telling where the sacrilege would stop.

So far, only the smaller churches had been seriously damaged. There was no guarantee that cathedrals were immune.

At that moment, a man of medium height and build was sitting at a kneehole desk in a large room in a flat overlooking Westminster Cathedral. There was coffee and toast on a tray at his left hand and a book open in front of him. The book, entitled *The Churches of London*, was open at the E section. In red ink, he placed a tick against St. Ethelreda's, Wembley, and then turned the pages to the G section, and ticked of St. Giles, Camberwell. Next he marked St. Olaf's, Charlton, and finally St. Colomb's, Putney. He was a pale, thin-faced man, with bony hands and anemic-looking fingernails; the ink showed up darkly against an almost transparent colorlessness.

In all, there were two thousand churches, chapels, and synagogues listed, under the headings:

Church of England
Roman Catholic
Free Churches
Foreign Churches
Synagogues

Of the two thousand, only the four now marked off and St. Denys, Kensington, were ticked. He ran his eye down each list until his pen came to rest at St. Paul's Cathedral. The pen hovered, then moved down a line to St. Paul's, Clapham, and he wrote the name of this on a slip of paper, then seven more church names, each on a separate slip. He took eight plain envelopes from a drawer in the desk and addressed each to a different man, at an address in London. He slipped the names of the churches in these envelopes, sealed and stamped them.

Not once did he smile; not once did he pause on his way to a post box opposite the tall red tower of the Cathedral.

CHAPTER 13
ANXIETY

Gideon knew that it would not be long before Scott-Marle wanted to know more about the raids on the churches and expected an urgent call from the Dean of St. Ludd's. He ran through the reports which had accumulated during the night and that morning, then called Hobbs, who was still in his office on the floor above.

"Come down, Alec, will you."

"Yes, at once." Hobbs never wasted a word.

He was in Gideon's office less than five minutes later, alert-looking, immaculate as ever, somehow very different from any other detective Gideon had known. He managed to make Gideon feel momentarily ill at ease.

"I'd like you to do the briefing again," Gideon said, and handed three files across his desk. "Seen Rollo's latest?"

"No."

"Henry Rhodes was shot in the back. There'll be a post mortem this morning but Rollo says the wound was the cause of death. Signs of a motorcycle which had stood in a hedge near the gate where the body was found are the only clue. A little oil had leaked—Castrol 30. Rollo's down at Southend, and Golightly's handling the London end. The most important thing is to find out whether Sally Dalby visited Rhodes, and whether hers is one of the photographs on the cellar walls. Also, we want to interview the girl friend in whom Sally Dalby confided that she was going to model for a photographer." Gideon paused, Hobbs nodded, and Gideon said, "All the rest speak for themselves."

"One thing," Hobbs said.

"Yes?"

"Golightly wants to know whether you want Entwhistle pulled in yet, or let him sweat."

"Nothing else in?"

"No."

"Let him sweat," Gideon said.

In fact, Entwhistle was sleeping off the whisky.

Eric Greenwood, in a much brighter frame of mind, reached the office of Cox and Shielding earlier than usual, even before Bessie Smith. He dealt with a lot of shipments which he had neglected the day before, from Persian and Indian carpets to Chinese jade and rose quartz, ivory from Hong Kong and opals from Australia. When Bessie came in, nose and cheeks an innocent gloss, he dictated at twice his usual speed. Twenty-five minutes later he said, "That's the lot, Bessie."

"I must say it's plenty," she said complainingly. "And I'm not at my brightest this morning."

"You look fine," Greenwood said heartily. "What's the trouble?"

"I was up half the night, with—"

"I didn't think it of you," Greenwood interrupted with pretended shock.

Bessie sniggered dutifully. "As a matter of fact, the church opposite me was one of the four that were damaged last night —you know, St. Ethelreda's. Did you read about it?"

Greenwood said, "No, I've hardly looked at my newspaper." He opened it, and read the headlines:

POLICEMAN BLINDED IN CHURCH EXPLOSION FOUR ALTARS BLOWN UP

He scowled, his lips set tightly, and there was righteous anger in his eyes.

"The sons of Satan," he said hotly.

"They're devils, that's what they are," muttered Bessie. "Why on earth would anyone want to do such a thing? And where will they strike next, that's what *I* want to know. The police don't seem to have a clue."

"The police? They're no damned good," Greenwood said.

He did not even look to see if there was anything new in the paper about Margaret Entwhistle's death; it was almost as if he felt that he had received absolution, and the burden and the fear of his crime had been taken from him.

In the course of the morning, most of the department managers mentioned the church explosions. . . .

In fact, during that morning, most of London talked about them. Overnight, it seemed, Londoners had become more church-conscious than they had been for fifty years. The blinding of the P.C. Davies was mentioned with horrified sympathy, while the sacrilege at the churches was discussed with shock, shame, or anger. Vergers, priests, and churchwardens found their aisles thronged, the clink and rustle of money going into the offertory boxes was trebled and quadrupled, and churches which seldom saw a visitor had many throughout the day. The damaged churches were besieged with newspapermen and tourists.

At Wembley Hospital, Mrs. Davies sat and waited for news of the operation which would mean life or death to her husband. Her children were with their grandmother.

At Lewisham, Entwhistle's mother-in-law had her grandchildren with her.

At their small suburban house, Sally Dalby's mother and father were answering the questions which Golightly put to them.

All over London, the work of the police went on; and at Scotland Yard, Gideon, Lemaitre and Dean Howcroft met together in Gideon's room.

Howcroft looked older and more frail.

Lemaitre, his eyes glassy and red-rimmed, had shaved, changed his shirt, and put on a blue and white spotted bow tie. He managed to look almost fresh.

Gideon, direct from Scott-Marle's office, was at his grimmest.

"We do feel that some degree of priority is required for these crimes," the Dean said, a note of reproof in his voice. "Unless we are assured you can give that we shall be very anxious indeed."

"If you'd come to us weeks ago we might have found out enough to have stopped it," Gideon remarked. "As it is, I think we've a major crisis on our hands. It will certainly get priority."

The Dean, rebuked, spread his pale, brown-spotted hands.

"The obvious question is—which church or churches next," Gideon went on. "Lemaitre is organizing the closest possible watch, but every church can't be protected all the time without a lot of help."

Lemaitre put in, "All the church authorities are being co-operative."

Gideon nodded, and waited.

"What we can't find is a common factor which might help us to anticipate the next churches likely to suffer," Lemaitre said. "We've had a High Church, two Low Church Anglicans, a Roman Catholic and a Wesleyan. They've nothing in common in antiquity: one was built three hundred years ago, one only twenty-two years. They don't seem to have a thing in common except that they're churches."

"Christian churches," amended Dean Howcroft mildly.

"Of course they're Christian, what else—" Lemaitre began, then stopped abruptly.

Gideon asked sharply, "What do you mean, Dean Howcroft?"

Again the old man spread his hands. "I was simply being specific," he said. "The churches you mentioned are Christian."

"Meaning, they're not Jewish synagogues."

"As you say, yes."

"Nor are they Moslem mosques or Hindu temples," Gideon went on. He looked forbidding, almost menacing. "I hope you won't make a remark like that in the hearing of the Press."

"My dear Commander, I stated a fact."

"In a way which could be construed to carry an implication against the Jews or other religions," said Gideon. "We've had far too much anti-Semitism in London. It's died down a lot, and we don't want it revived."

Lemaitre fidgeted uncomfortably, sensing a conflict but unable to do a thing about it. Gideon, huge compared with the Dean, florid against the other's pinkish pallor and silky white halo, sat glowering. The Dean met his gaze squarely, sternly unrepentant.

Utterly at a loss, Lemaitre said tentatively, "Everyone's talking about it."

"Of course they are," said Gideon. "That is why we don't want the wrong kind of slant."

The Dean drew a long, slow breath. "Commander, I hope you are not refusing to consider every possibility?"

"All we can see are being considered."

"I'm very glad to hear it. There *is* such a thing as anti-Semitism. And there are among the Jews young and fanatical individuals who hate the Christian church for it, just as there are fanatical, anti-Semitic Christians. We are not yet in an age of full religious tolerance."

Gideon said, "There's a lot of bitterness between High Church and Low in the Church of England. There are extremists in the Church of England as well as in the Roman Catholic Church. One group is no more suspect than another. If the Press gets hold of a remark like yours they may twist and distort it. Even a whisper could start a wave of religious hatred that could do great harm. Surely you can see *that*."

Lemaitre had never seen Gideon so plainly angry, and now he kept silent, knowing that there was nothing he could usefully do.

The Dean said, "Yes, Commander, I can indeed."

"Then why—" Gideon began.

"Forgive me," interrupted the Dean in a voice in which Gideon's forgiveness seemed the very last thing for which he craved. "Perhaps my remark may be easier to accept if I explain at once that it was in fact a quotation from one of your own officers, heard this morning."

Gideon felt as if he had been flung against a wall, the impact of that statement was so great. Lemaitre pressed his hands against his damp forehead. For a few seconds, no one spoke. Eventually, the Dean broke the silence.

"Commander, if we cannot solve this mystery quickly, there will be no stopping rumor of every kind. I am only too keenly aware that you should have been informed before, and deplore the fact that you were not. But—forgive me again—we have to deal with the situation as it is, not as it should be. Is there any clue?"

"None yet," Gideon said, gruffly.

"I wouldn't say that," protested Lemaitre. "We know where the dynamite's made. We're on the ball there all right. We simply lack the motive."

"Superintendent," said the Dean, "there is no fanatic more dangerous than the religious fanatic. As Mr. Gideon has reminded us, there has been a long period of quiet on the issue of religious tolerance. This could bring that period abruptly to an end."

Gideon said, "Dean Howcroft, are you being wholly frank?"

"In what way?"

"Do you have any reason to believe this is being done to stir up religious fanaticism?"

"I have no reason to believe it at all. It is an obvious possibility, however. The newspapers won't fail to point it out, and gossip and rumor are no doubt already busy with it. If this were not enough, our churches, perhaps some of our most historic churches, are in danger of serious damage." He paused, leaned forward, and asked earnestly, "Are you *sure* that nothing more can be done to find the perpetrators? Watching and guarding the churches is essential, of course, and invaluable—but the real preventative will be to remove the danger."

When the Dean had gone, Lemaitre looked at Gideon's set face and said uneasily, "The old man talks a lot, but he's no fool."

"No," agreed Gideon dryly. "And no one's going to agree with the last half of your sentence more heartily than he will.

But we've got to pull out all the stops, Lem. Not being a fool isn't enough to produce the culprits. I saw the Commissioner this morning, and the Lords Spiritual are beginning to chase the Home Secretary, who is beginning to chase us. We've got a really ugly situation on our hands. If you can solve this one quickly—"

"I'll solve it," Lemaitre interrupted, with a confidence he could not justify. "Don't you worry, George. I'll solve it."

When he had gone, in turn, Gideon wondered for the first time whether it had been a mistake to give this case to Lemaitre. Overconfidence could be disastrous.

Toni Bottelli was overconfident, too.

He felt quite sure that he had not been seen and recognized, because he had traveled to Southend from London on one motorcycle, a BSA, and from the rendezvous on the Honda, wearing helmet and goggles. The Honda machine was in a village car park and could not be connected with him or the murder; someone would come and collect it in a few days. There was nothing to worry about, no direct association between his photographic studio cellar in Tottenham and the one in Fulham from which Rhodes had been driven.

So he could go back to Sally Dalby.

He did not know himself really well, but there were things he did recognize; among them the fact that certain girls had a fascination for him. He wanted to dominate them absolutely, wanted to make them do everything and anything he desired. He did not know why he felt that way about one girl in twenty or so, he was only very sure that that was the way he felt. Twenty would look more or less alike, their measurements wouldn't greatly vary, but one of them would have the quality that mesmerized him. Until she was virtually his slave, he could not look at anyone else. Once he had a girl completely under his thumb, she lost her attraction. Three of them had been so appalled and horrified at the lengths to which he had gone that they had threatened to tell the police.

So he had poisoned them with Veronal; and they had died.

Now he was going back to his latest "slave," Sally. Sally was still attractive to him; he had brilliantly circumvented any danger which might have spread from Harry Rhodes and could concentrate with an easy mind on the girl.

CHAPTER 14
"I WANT TO GO HOME"

"I want to go home," Sally said.

"What's the matter with this place?" Bottelli asked. "Isn't it grand enough?"

"It's lovely, but I want to go home."

"Why can't you be at home here?"

"It isn't the same," insisted Sally.

She sat up in a big bed, looking almost incredibly attractive, her hair falling in golden strands to her shoulders, her eyes only just touched with eye shadow, her naturally curling lashes very slightly darkened, her complexion wholly without blemish. She wore a frilly bed jacket, high at the neck, and the pillows behind her were downy and luxurious. The bedspread was of a very pale pink. Opposite her and on each wall were huge mirrors, from which one could see reflections at every conceivable angle.

Toni sat on the side of the bed, very handsome, dark and swarthy. He was not annoyed or angry, but in a teasing mood, knowing exactly what he wanted. He knew too that the drugs would gradually weaken her resistance, until a moment would come when she would be wholly compliant.

"I should think it's not the same," he said. "This is luxury, you live in the slums."

"Oh, I don't!" she protested.

"Not far off," he said. "Have you got a room of your own?"

"Well, no, but—"

"You share it with little sister Mary," he reminded her. "She's a school kid who throws her clothes all over the place, uses your lipstick and powder and borrows your stockings. Remember?"

"Well, she *is* my sister."

"And she gets under your feet all the time."

Sally looked at him steadily and soberly, and then said, "I don't care what you say, I want to go home."

"Okay, so you shall—one of these days."

"No—today."

He stood up, half frowning, half smiling. Looking up at

him Sally was a little frightened, and at the same time a little admiring; he *was* so good-looking. She wondered if she had made him angry, while in rather a vague way she associated him with pain.

"I'll see what I can do," he promised. He moved toward the door, then hesitated, came back to the bed and selected a chocolate from a rich-looking box at the bedside. He bit into it appreciatively. "Like one?"

"They're lovely."

"They're the best—only the best is good enough for you!"

She chose one with a nut on top, as he knew she would; and she would eat several more, now she had started. In each was a grain of hashish, which would make her forget all about that tiresome desire to go home. Her fears and tensions would relax and she would do whatever he wanted.

He knew, because she already had.

He knew, also, because there were three other girls to remember, all of whom had become compliant after eating those chocolates while reclining in that bed.

Golightly entered the supermarket where a girl named Daphne Arnold worked, walked past the bright stacks of tinned and packet foods, past bread and cheese in great variety, past meat and pies displayed at the delicatessen counter, and finally reached the office marked MANAGER. A surprisingly youthful man looked up with irritable preoccupation and demanded, "What can I do for you?"

"I'd like to see Miss Arnold," Golightly said.

"The staff can't be spared for private matters in business hours."

Golightly simply took out and proffered his card. The young man's manner changed at once. He sprang up and with a murmured apology hurried out, calling sharply, "Miss Arnold—wanted at the office, please."

A girl approached from one of the counters. She had an exaggerated mop of black hair, a snub nose and a figure which managed to overcome the disadvantage of a mass-produced, dark blue smock. She looked at Golightly demurely.

"Yes, Mr. Smith?"

"This gentleman would like a word with you. I'll be in the storeroom." The manager went out abruptly, while Golightly waited for the girl to drop her gaze.

"You're a friend of Sally Dalby," Golightly said at last.

"Yes, that's right."

"She told you she was going to pose as a photographer's model."

"Yes, that's right."

"Do you know where she was going to pose for him?"

"No, I don't."

"Did she say anything more about it?"

"No, she didn't."

"Would you like to come along to the police station for a few hours, until you've recovered your memory?"

The girl's eyes rounded with alarm. "No! *I* haven't done anything!"

"Sure about that?" asked Golightly. He let his gaze move about the supermarket, at the cash desks and the crowded shelves, looked back at her, and went on. "What else did Sally tell you about this photographer?"

"Not much," Daphne Arnold said.

"How much? Let's stop wasting time."

"All I know is that she said his name was Toni," answered Daphne with a rush. "But she made me promise not to tell anyone, because if her father knew, he would be hopping mad. That's the truth—I *promised* her."

"What else did you promise not to tell anyone?" Golightly demanded.

"Nothing, really. She'd been to see this feller once, and she told me what the place was like." Boldness crept back into the girl's eyes and manner and confidence returned with it. "She said there were hundreds and hundreds of photographs around the walls, she wasn't the only one to be photographed without any clothes. There was nothing to be ashamed of, she said. Her figure was as good as anyone's there."

"Did you ever see this Toni?"

"No. I swear I didn't."

"Did she ever talk about meeting other people with him?"

"No, she wanted to keep him to her herself."

"Why?"

"He was ever so handsome, she told me," Daphne said. Her expression changed again and her voice rose. "He was an Italian, or a Spaniard, or something like that."

Golightly felt that he had made quite a step forward.

When he felt sure there was nothing else that the girl could tell him, he went straight from the supermarket to the street of small, terraced houses where Sally Dalby lived. Her father was a sign painter who worked in a shed in the back yard. Her mother was a gray, fluffy, vague individual, on whom nothing seemed to make an impression.

"Oh, it's another policeman . . . Come about Sally, I dare say . . . You haven't found her, I suppose? . . . No, well, I expect she'll turn up one day, like a bad penny . . . Yes, my hubby's in, will you come through?"

He followed her through the house to a shed which smelled of potatoes, paint, and varnish. The whole of one wall was of glass, and crowding the others were half-finished paintings in vivid and striking colors. A stack of gilt picture framing was piled in one corner beside a bench crammed with pots of paint and half-filled jars of brushes. On another bench were some inn signs and notices, all boldly and effectively done.

Dalby was a short, stubby-haired man; a hedgehog of a man.

"Where's the detective who usually comes to see me?" he demanded suspiciously.

"Following another angle," Golightly told him smoothly. "Mr. Dalby, has your daughter ever talked to you about a man named Toni?"

"No."

"Did you know she was interested in posing for a photographer?"

"If I'd known, I'd have had the hide off her."

"I see," said Golightly. Rollo had told him that talking to Dalby was like talking to a brick wall, and he began to understand what his colleague meant. "Have you had any message at all from or about her?"

"If I had, I would have told you," Dalby stated.

Golightly looked at him steadily, nodded, and turned away. As he reached the door he heard a movement behind him, but he did not turn round until he was halfway to the back door of the little house.

"Superintendent," Dalby called.

"Yes?"

"Find her, for God's sake find her," Dalby pleaded in a desperate voice. "And tell her she can come back. Whatever she's done. I won't take it out of her. You must make her believe that."

Golightly thought, but is it true? and turned to face this man squarely, the question on the tip of his tongue. He did not say it, however; he needed no telling at all that at the moment Dalby's whole being was in the words he had uttered, that he was flagellating himself because of a sense of guilt at having driven his daughter away.

"We will do everything we can," Golightly promised.

As he drove off, he wondered what would happen in this strange household if he had to report that the girl had been murdered.

About the time that Golightly drove away from the Dalby house, Rollo entered the laboratory at Southend Police Headquarters to talk to the pathologist, who had finished the autopsy on Rhodes. Eric Greenwood was walking up the gangway of a ship which had brought a special cargo of llama wool from South America. Entwhistle was making himself some strong coffee. Mrs. Davies was waiting for the verdict as two surgeons fought to save her husband's life. The Dean of St. Ludd's was entering the main gates of Lambeth Palace to report to the Bishop; while Elspeth Chaplin watched her grandfather's pale face and pain-racked eyes, sharing his distress at the damage to the church he loved.

While all these things took place, part of the surging, throbbing vitality of London's life, while the police and the transport men and in fact all of London's eight million human beings went about their business, Lemaitre stepped out of his car outside the last of the churches to be damaged. Along the road there was a branch post office, and letters were being left there for sorting before the next morning's delivery.

Among the letters being carried in a big sack was one posted by the man whose flat overlooked Westminster Cathedral. Oblivious of this, as the police must be of so many crimes in their incipient stage, Lemaitre went into the Roman Catholic Church of St. Augustine, Maida Vale. The routine work was finished and much tidying up had already been done. Eight or nine men were busy among the litter caused by the explosion, and one of them turned and limped toward Lemaitre. This was Father Devan, a priest well known because of his television appeals for charity. He was a round, chubby-faced man, with merry eyes; bald, rather portly, and distinctly rubicund. His voice was clear and beautifully modulated.

"Hallo, sir. How can I help you?"

"I'm Superintendent Lemaitre, from Scotland Yard."

"Oh, I heard you would be coming, Superintendent. May I say how appreciative we are of the consideration of the police."

"We do what we can," Lemaitre said. "Can you spare me ten minutes?"

"Of course. My study will be the best place." Father Devan led the way toward the side of the church. Passing the workers he went out to a house almost adjoining and took Lemaitre into a small room with a table, two chairs a crucifix, some books, and on one side, some manuscript paper and a quill pen. Lemaitre noticed that there were illuminations on the manuscript pages. Seeing the way he glanced, Father Devan said, "I've a great love for illustrated manuscripts, and it's always been my hope to transcribe the Bible in my own hand." He motioned to a chair. "Please sit down."

Lemaitre could not resist picking up a sheet of the paper, scrutinizing the immaculate Old English lettering and the red, green, and gilt scroll at the top. "That's really good," he said with feeling. "If I weren't a flatfoot I'd like to be an etcher. Like to see what I mean?" He took out his wallet, selected a slip of paper, and handed it across the desk, grinning broadly. Father Devan unfolded it, his eyes widening. "How about that!"

"It's a five-pound note," the parish priest observed.

"All my own work," Lamaitre boasted. "Good job I was born on the right side of the law, isn't it?" He waited for a few moments while the other pored over his forgery, then went on. "Did it for a joke." He took it back, shedding hilarity, becoming at once deeply grave. "The truth is, padre, I'm worried stiff over these explosions. Never know what'll go next—look bad if they blew up Poet's Corner in the Abbey, or the Nelson catafalque in the crypt at St. Paul's, wouldn't it?"

"It would be a disaster," agreed Father Devan.

"Be a disaster for me, too," said Lemaitre. "This is one job I mustn't fall down on."

"How can I help?" asked Devan.

"What I'm looking for is a common denominator," Lemaitre explained. "Anything in common among all the damaged churches in this part of London. I've got a list here—seven R.C. churches and twenty-three Anglican—"

"As many as that!" exclaimed Devan.

"Yes, for a start." Lemaitre opened his briefcase and put a sheet of paper in front of the priest. "There's the list, and I want to find out if *you* have anything in common with them. Apart from Christianity, I mean, and that's not the point. Do you know of anything you have in common?"

Devan ran his eye down the lists, then slowly shook his head. "I can think of nothing."

"Tell you what I want you to do," said Lemaitre, as if confiding in a bosom friend. "Go through that list with a tooth-comb and put down if you've ever visited them—whether you know the priest in charge, anything at all to show a connection. And then I'd like you to make out a list of all your associated groups, clubs, societies, mission stations—every possible bit of information you have. I'm going to get a list from every church and try to find that connection. Tell you one possibility."

"Oh. What is it?" inquired Devan.

"Someone who hates the ecumenical idea. You or anyone at the church have anything special to do with that?"

"Not as far as I know. There are, of course, my television appeals, but the causes are too widely divergent to be the reason of a specific animosity. However, I will certainly do what you ask to find out any association, any activity—such as service on charity committees and community efforts—which we might share with these other churches."

"And let me know when you've finished, I'll get it collected," Lemaitre said. He stood up, and the priest followed suit, rather awkwardly. "Hurt your leg?" asked Lemaitre commiseratingly.

Devan smiled. "I left a piece of one behind in Normandy, on D day."

"Oh. Bloody bad luck," said Lemaitre, and added hastily, "Sorry, padre. Forgot where I was."

He strode out, cheered up by the interview. Though he had gained little, there was something about Devan's personality which appealed to him. As he settled into his car, he began to calculate how long it was likely to be before hearing from all the priests concerned.

"A couple of weeks, and we need results in a couple of days. What the hell's the use? If only those so-and-so parsons had let us know before."

That night, eight more churches were severely damaged.

CHAPTER 15
THE BISHOP'S PALACE

On the other side of the River Thames from New Scotland Yard, between Westminster and Lambeth Bridges, lay Lambeth Palace, the Archbishop's residence and the diocesan offices, where the business of much of the Church of England was carried out. Far less known than the Abbey, which lay between the two buildings, or the Roman Catholic Cathedral of Westminster, which was only a few hundred yards away, it nestled near the river bank, ancient and venerable as buildings go, under the shadow of the Houses of Parliament. Great decisions had been made in the palace during the Lambeth Conferences of all the Anglican Bishops throughout the world.

Almost exactly a hundred years ago the first of the con-
vocations had been held, with some dissidence and some
heart-searching. During the intervening years a host of sub-
jects had been discussed, many of them controversial, and
many recommendations had been made to the Privy Council
of the Church. In those early days the recommendations had
been cautious and had seldom carried great weight. Today,
decisions of the Conferences were of key importance in
Anglican affairs.

Every conceivable subject which might affect the welfare
of the Church and the health of Christianity had been discussed. Here were taken the first steps toward reunion with
those churches which had broken away centuries before. Here
successive Archbishops of Canterbury, their London home at
the Palace, made historic pronouncements on ecumenical
affairs, on marriage, divorce, on ritual, creed and dogma. No
change of any significance had ever occurred until it had
been discussed and deliberated upon in this place.

Not once in the history of the Palace, however, had an
issue been discussed involving Scotland Yard, and actual
crime.

There was an air almost of unreality among the five men
who gathered there on the afternoon when Lemaitre had
been boasting of his skill in forgery. The Archbishop of Canterbury was not in residence but had delegated his powers to
another Bishop, whose forbidding air was tempered by the
homeliness of steel-framd bifocal spectacles worn well down
on the bridge of his nose. Howcroft, Dean of St. Ludd's and
the group's liaison officer with the police, was at his right
hand. The Dean of the Abbey was next to him, a gentle-
looking ascetic with a mind known to be as decisive as a trap.
There was also a representative from the Free Church Council, William Steel, a well-known broadcaster and writer who
looked not unlike a popular actor of the times. The fifth man
was the Roman Catholic, Jonathan Northwick, the Administrator for the Cardinal, tall and patriarchal-looking. Thse five
were gathered about an oval table in a book-lined room overlooking a lawn so vividly green and velvet smooth that it
seemed more like baize than grass.

"Gentlemen," said the Bishop, "we all feel that the urgency
of the situation is so great that we should take emergency
measures—distressing though the situation is. As we have met
so often to discuss ways and means in which we can work
more closely together, I thought it advisable to meet, briefly,
before we are joined by others seldom in our councils. Seldom
indeed."

He paused, looking over his lenses at everyone present.

"I have, at the request of the Commissioner of the Metropolitan Police, invited the Chief Rabbi or his chosen representative, and also the Commander of the Criminal Investigation Department, whom some of you may know."

"Gideon," remarked Northwick. "A very sound man."

"I've met him," said Steel, briskly.

"Do we—ah—seriously fear that synagogues might also be affected?" asked the Bishop.

"The police think so," said Howcroft, as if that clinched the matter. "The only essential preliminary, as far as I can see, is that we should all be aware of the possibility of a worsening situation and the very real probability that the number of churches affected might increase quite alarmingly." He peered at the Dean of the Abbey, and paused.

"*Are* there any grounds for such theories?" the Dean wanted to know. "I am not being an obstructionist, you understand, but neither do I feel the need to be an alarmist."

"Do we know what Gideon will expect us to do?" asked Steel.

"Expect?" Northwick's eyebrows raised in surprise rather than disapproval.

The Bishop looked interrogatively at Dean Howcroft.

"I'm quite satisfied that Commander Gideon takes the matter very seriously and has it in proper perspective," the Dean declared. "I think we shall be well advised to be guided by him."

Before anyone could comment, there was a tap at the door. Dean Howcroft stood up and moved toward it as it opened. A very broad, thick-set man, Daniel Cohen, the Secretary of the London United Synagogues, came in. Gideon, much the same build but a head taller, followed. Howcroft led them to the table, and the Bishop introduced them amid a general shuffling of chairs and murmuring.

Gideon found himself next to Dean Howcroft.

"Now that we are all here," said the Bishop, "I'm sure I voice the sentiments of everyone present when I say how grateful we are to the police for their swift and ready cooperation."

There was more murmuring.

"Commander," went on the Bishop, "I wonder if you would care to make a statement on the situation as you see it at this moment."

Gideon, seldom in the slightest degree self-conscious, was a little embarrassed. He had never before been in Lambeth Palace, and there was something a little awesome—not about the building itself, but about its history and its traditions. He had a confusion of ideas, partly that this was rather like a prayer meeting, partly that he was very out of place. Even the other layman present habitually moved in a more rarefied religious atmosphere. Gideon was acutely conscious of his lack of knowledge of ecclesiastical modes and affairs. In a way he was glad that he was called on so quickly; he did not have time to worry.

"The situation as I see it now," he echoed, a little hoarsely. He coughed. "That needn't take much time, sir. I will say at once that the position appears to me to be of the utmost gravity. The incidents last night really alarmed us at the Yard. If I had my way, every church of every denomination would be placed under police guard until the problem is solved—but we haven't enough men to do it even in the Metropolitan area. So—we need your help."

"Ah," said the Abbey Dean.

"In what way?" demanded Northwick.

"Each church must have a watchman every hour of the day and night," said Gideon. "Something like the fireguards and the wardens during the war. You had then a team of over two hundred at St. Ludd's, and the Abbey had as many. You wouldn't, of course, need that number now, but every door needs watching. The churches and cathedrals will have to be kept under close surveillance during services to make sure no one stays behind. It has to be done quickly and thoroughly. I can make sure that there is at least one policeman on call all the time, and at the bigger churches I'll have a regular patrol. Flying Squad and patrol cars will be available at all hours. It will mean stretching our forces to their limit, and if we get a rash of other crimes we'll be in trouble, but this case has priority. We'll do our share—but our effort may well be wasted if you can't help substantially."

When he stopped speaking, the silence seemed to come from a group of men utterly appalled.

"*Can* it be so bad?" asked the Abbey Dean, obviously shocked but prepared to minimize the shock of others.

"I think so, sir."

"You mean you think that if we institute this guard, these —ah—vandals will exert themselves to circumvent it?"

"Yes, sir."

"It is quite easy to get round guards," Cohen said, almost dejectedly. "One man, one tiny object, little bigger than a matchstick—and a whole church can be destroyed, sacred objects ruined, the very sanctity of our beliefs violated. It can be done. The problem is constantly with us, and our congregations already form patrols. The Board of Directors of British Jews has the problem continually under review." He gave a grim smile. "Ask any Hindu what can happen to his gods, and any Muslim what can happen to the Koran."

"So you are accustomed to these attacks," Northwick said uncomfortably. "I hadn't realized it was so bad in the synagogues."

"Few people do, except the police," said Cohen.

"The point is, can you all do what I ask?" Gideon said authoritatively.

"Not immediately, I fear," answered the Bishop. "It certainly cannot be done tonight. A start might be made, but no more. By tomorrow night we could have a greater number of churches protected."

Gideon looked at Northwick. "And you, sir?"

"The same applies, although perhaps on a slightly quicker scale. The Catholic Police Guild—"

"You won't get much help from them, sir," Gideon interspersed bluntly. "All the members will be on overtime or standing by for extra duty."

Northwick said, "Oh, of course. All the same, we can call on the St. Vincent de Paul Brothers, or the Legion of Mary. Yes, you can rely on us."

"I'm very glad. And you, Mr. Steel?"

"The big churches, yes," answered the Freechurchman promptly. "The smaller ones—membership and workers are so pathetically small, but—yes, we can make a start." He rubbed his chin. "The mechanics of the situation are difficult in themselves. How can we get messages—" He broke off, forcing a laugh, and went on. "I am sorry. This has put me off my stroke. I will arrange for an Action Committee to start telephoning our clergy at once. That is—" he glanced sharply round at the others—"if we all agree that it is necessary."

Northwick said, "It seems we have no choice."

"Yes, I suppose it is inevitable," said the Abbey Dean reluctantly.

"The wording of our message—I wonder if we are underrating the difficulties," Dean Howcroft murmured, the lines of his face falling into folds of age and barely tolerated resignation.

Gideon, deeply relieved, opened a small briefcase and took out some typewritten pages. He passed these round from hand to hand so that everyone had a copy, and there were several left over.

"We had this memorandum prepared today, gentlemen. If you care to approve or amend it, we can have sufficient copies printed for one or two to go to every church secretary— or leader, or vicar, or priest," he added hurriedly, conscious of the sensitivity of dogmatic toes. "Anyone who has authority to act, that is. And we can distribute them to our divisional stations and substations and have them delivered from there. Each Division knows the person to consult about each local church."

The Bishop said with rare warmth, "We are indeed indebted to you."

Gideon felt almost triumphant as the silence settled after the murmur of assent, and all fell to reading the memorandum he had prepared early that afternoon:

TO ALL CHURCH, CHAPEL
AND SYNAGOGUE OFFICIALS
URGENT NOTICE

Willful damage to churches and church property is being carried out by a number of persons with obvious malice. The Metropolitan Police have reason to believe that every place of worship in the London area may be in danger.

Small but highly dangerous charges of high explosive can easily be left in pews, fonts, carvings, candlesticks or holders, and elsewhere. They can be left behind by individuals under the guise of worshipers or tourists.

For the safety of your church we strongly recommend that you institute an exhaustive search as soon as possible. The local police will assist you in this but the manpower necessary must be mainly from church members and officials.

It is also strongly recommended that *all* doors are locked at dusk until this period of emergency is over. A night watch, on the lines of fire-watching during the Second World War, is also strongly recommended. Police officers will always be near at hand and police reinforcements will be readily available.

It is impossible to stress the importance of these precautions too strongly. Eleven churches have now suffered serious damage.

Signed:

The Dean of St. Paul's—For the City of London
The Dean of the Abbey—For the City of Westminster
Jonathan Northwick   —For the Cardinal Bishop of
                                    Westminster

The Dean of St. Ludd's	—For Anglican Churches in Greater London
John Steel	—For the Free Church Council
Daniel Cohen	—For the London United Synagogue

Within two hours of Gideon's return to the Yard the notices were speeding on their way.

At the same time, church members and church workers were homeward bound from shops and offices, factories and warehouses, from the countless little businesses which made up commercial London. Office managers and typists, sales girls and models, directors and janitors, doorkeepers and salesmen—all of these and many others, on reaching home, were called out by their church and asked to serve.

Almost without exception, they agreed; men and women, shocked and angry, ready to defend that which was of paramount importance to their way of life.

As darkness fell, half of the churches of London were fully protected.

That night, not a single church was attacked.

CHAPTER 16
A PROBLEM IN FRAUD

Lemaitre, looking much fresher after a full and undisturbed night's sleep, breezed into Gideon's office with a perfunctory tap and spoke even before Gideon looked up. It was a perfect morning. The blue of the sky was clear and vivid and the shimmering of the sun's reflection on the river touched the windows of the office and played, like a shadow dancing, on the glass of a photograph of the cricket team of the Metropolitan Police taken twenty years before.

"Good morning, George! We've stopped the baskets."

Gideon went on writing, merely grunting, "What's that?"

"I said we'd stopped the baskets." Lemaitre, conscious of an implied rebuff, hovered in front of the desk. He was so smooth-shaven that his skin was shining, his hair so pomaded that it looked like the painted head of a Dutch doll.

Gideon, studying the latest reports on the photo-nudes murder case and glum because Sally Dalby had not been found, felt a flash of exasperation which was not far from annoyance at Lemaitre's facile optimism, but he checked the expression of it as he looked up.

"Or they stopped themselves."

"Doesn't make much difference, so long as they've stopped," said Lemaitre, and then went on earnestly, "I didn't mean we'd finished altogether, George, even I'm not such a silly beggar as to think that. I mean we stopped 'em for last night, and that's given us a breathing space." He paused, obviously hoping that his words carried conviction.

Gideon thought suddenly that for all these years he might have been taking Lemaitre's overoptimism too seriously. The thought died away in the realization that in fact Lemaitre was at last trying to correct this deeply implanted habit.

"Yes, and we can use the breathing space," Gideon said. "What we need to know is how many churches are properly guarded."

"I've got a system," Lemaitre declared.

Gideon suppressed a snort of amusement; it was too frivolous for the occasion.

"I can't get out to all the Divisions," Lemaitre continued importantly. "I'd need to cut myself in pieces to see the lot. But they can come *here*. So if you'll call all the Divisional Supers in for two-thirty, say, I could brief 'em. *They* can check how the churches are being protected, what kind of response the memo's had, and they can tell me—us I mean—of any weak spots. We can then get to work on the bloody Bishops."

Gideon found himself laughing. "Call the Divisional Superintendents in if you want to," he said, glancing at his watch. "It's only nine-fifteen. No reason why they shouldn't be here by half-past eleven. Send out a teletype request, sign it for me. Use the main lecture room. Let 'em know what it's about so that they will bring all the information we need."

Lemaitre's eyes were glowing. "Right away, George!" He strode out, let the door slam, opened it again and said, "Sorry!" breezily, and went out with hardly a sound.

Gideon sat thinking for a few moments. Lemaitre's very heart was in this job; he saw it as a way to justify himself completely in his own eyes because he had been passed over for Hobbs. His enthusiasm and his eagerness were infectious, but if he should fail he would find it a bitter and, in its way, a killing blow.

Was he, Gideon, exaggerating?

He pushed the thought aside and rang for the Chief Inspector who was standing in for Lemaitre.

"Who's waiting to see me?"

"Mr. Rollo, sir, Mr. Golightly, and Mr. Simmons."

"I'll see Mr. Simmons first, then the others together."

"Right, sir!"

"Is Mr. Hobbs in?"

"No, sir. There was a message. I didn't take it myself, but I heard about it. His wife's very ill, sir."

"Oh. Yes." Gideon nodded, and added, "Ask Mr. Simmons to come in five minutes." He picked up the outside telephone. "Get my wife for me, please." He rang off, and almost immediately the internal telephone rang, and he picked up the receiver. "Gideon."

"Commander," said Scott-Marle, abruptly, "I have the Governor of the Bank of England in my office."

Gideon thought quickly, "Should I know what this is about?" He could recall nothing.

The Commissioner went on. "He has some reason for anxiety about gold losses—very serious gold losses—in shipments between here and South Africa and Australia, as well as international shipments between several countries."

This was abosolutely new to Gideon and the thought of it made everything else fade from his mind—even the attacks on the churches. Such losses must be on a big scale if the Governor of the Bank of England was at the Yard in person.

"How long has he known about this?" Gideon asked.

"A day or two. It has to be kept quiet for the time being, but there will have to be a conference of senior police officers and senior customs officers of the countries concerned. I would like you and the Commander of the Special Branch to attend the conference, which will be held in Paris on Tuesday and Wednesday next. I know you are deeply involved in current affairs, but this is unavoidable."

Gideon said, "I can see that, sir."

"Officially the conference will be on drugs," the Commissioner went on. "In fact the only subject will be the gold bullion problem. Will you arrange to go and see the Governor some time today or tomorrow and discuss it with him?"

"Certainly," promised Gideon. "Do you say he's with you now?"

"Yes."

"Would this afternoon be convenient for him?"

There was a murmur in the background before Scott-Marle spoke again.

"Half-past three, at the Athenaeum Club. He will be in the library."

"I'll be there," said Gideon.

As he rang off the door opened and Chief Superintendent Simmons came in. Simmons looked a little like a lecherous Punch, and the fact that he was the cleanest-living man imaginable did not lessen that impression. Behind a jocund leeriness, however, lay one of the keenest minds at the Yard. He was a mathematician and an accountant, and no one in England knew more about company law. For over five weeks, now, he had been investigating the activities of a company which controlled dozens of subsidiary companies, among all of which there was reason to suspect enormous tax evasion. There was also reason to suspect a major case of share-pushing.

"Sit down," Gideon said.

"Thanks." Simmons looked at Gideon searchingly, and then said in a rather grating voice, "Heard any good sermons lately?"

Gideon chuckled. "Any ideas about that job?"

"Haven't given it a thought," said Simmons. "Hope the beggars don't have a go at St. Paul's or the Abbey, that's all." He paused.

"So do I. What have you got?"

"Trouble and worry," answered Simmons. "I'm not sure there's a case for the Public Prosecutor—certainly there isn't yet, and finding out for sure whether it's a civil or a criminal case will take another four weeks of solid going."

"Think it's worth four weeks?"

"It is to me. It is to Inland Revenue—their Investigation Branch really thinks they're onto outsize evasion. It's borderline, mind you—very clever accountants on the other side, but there may be a share-pushing angle as well as tax evasion. The thing is—" He paused.

"What other job have I got for you?" suggested Gideon.

"That, and—should we leave it to the Inland Revenue and only come in if they can hand us share-pushing on a plate?"

"How long will the Inland Revenue chaps take?"

"Another year, at the present rate of progress. They'd like us to keep on too, of course."

"I dare say they would," remarked Gideon dryly. "That way they would get half their work done for them." He watched the faint reflection from river and window play on the back of his hand, then looked straight at Simmons. "If the parent company promotes any more smaller companies, it could fleece a lot of people in a year, couldn't it?"

"It certainly could." Simmons's corrugated forehead looked almost smooth for a moment. "Do we want to risk it?"

"No. Keep at it. If it looks like keeping you busy for more

than a month, let me know. Have you got all the help you need?"

"Yes, thanks."

"That's something," said Gideon.

When the door had closed on Simmons he opened the fraud case file, made a note, pondered for a few moments, then closed it. He brought out an empty manila folder and made some penciled notes on the inside of the cover. They ran:

B of E. Bullion.
What countries besides G.B., S.A. and Aust'a?
Athenaeum, 3.30, today.
Check flights to Paris after seeing Gov. He may have something planned.

He closed the folder, knowing that there was a real possibility of a major investigation over the gold, wishing he knew more about it and also wishing that it hadn't come at this juncture. There could be ugly developments at the churches by Monday or Tuesday, and he would have preferred to stay in England. Hobbs would have to take over, and he wasn't too keen on Hobbs and Lemaitre working together on this particular investigation—Lemaitre might be far too sensitive. Then he thought, Dammit, I asked for Kate. He lifted the outside telephone as the door opened to admit Rollo and Golightly. He waved to chairs as he said, "What happened to that call to my wife? . . . Yes, keep trying." He rang off and looked into the faces of these two officers who were so different and yet could work together as an excellent team. Rollo looked as vigorous and healthy as ever, ten years younger than his age; Golightly had an air which suggested that butter wouldn't melt in his mouth.

Neither looked particularly pleased, though Rollo never found it easy to hide elation.

"Who's going to start?" asked Gideon.

"There isn't another clue in the Rhodes murder," Rollo announced. "We haven't found the motorcycle, haven't discovered where Rhodes holed up, haven't found any of his associates. He did this job at the chemist's, and was competent enough. The cellar was a spare-time and evening occupation. Percy did spot one thing that I missed."

Gideon turned his gaze on Golightly.

"The photographs on the wall of Rhodes's cellar were all printed off the same kind of negative," he said, "and printed on the same kind of paper and in the same type of solution. We're checking photographic suppliers."

"Couldn't Rhodes have supplied the stuff?"

"The paper he used in the printing at the chemist's is a poorer quality than that of the cellar photographs," Golightly stated. "The cellar ones are all printed on Kodak Bromesko, a white, smooth, glossy paper, and all developed by a good, high-definition developer from a fine-grain film. I'd say a very good camera was used, German or Japanese. All of the prints were obviously handled by someone wearing rubber gloves— quite common in the developing process—and there are no prints except Rhodes's."

Gideon said, "And the Dalby girl?"

"Vanished without a trace."

"This Italian or Spaniard whom the girl at the supermarket talked about?"

"No line on him yet."

Gideon was still watching the flickering on the back of his hand. "Has the time come to try to get in touch with all girls who pose for photographers and see if they know about this man?"

"That's the rub," said Rollo.

"No need to be obscure," rebuked Gideon.

"Sorry. These aren't regular models. I've been to twenty photographers who specialize in nudes and none of them admits to recognizing any of the girls. I've tried every art and model agency in London, too. Rhodes and this good-looking Toni used amateurs—and so far we haven't found any of the girls he used."

Gideon said, "Dammit. How many have been reported missing? Thirty?"

"Thirty-two."

"And we can't even find one of those?"

"Just the three dead ones," Rollo reminded him. "Rhodes had their photographs all right."

There was a moment of absolute silence, so acute, so profound and searching, that it was almost as if all three men had stopped breathing at the same moment; after a few seconds, all of them began to breathe again, a little stiffly and with an effort.

Gideon said, "Are you seriously telling me you think *all* the other girls have been murdered?"

Rollo shifted in his chair, and began to speak at the same moment as Golightly.

"I know it sounds crazy—"

"It may seem ludicrous—"

They both came to an abrupt halt.

"When did you start thinking like this?" demanded Gideon.

"Idea struck me last night," said Rollo. "Percy and I had a talk on the telephone."

"It hit me like a sledgehammer," Golightly put in.

"It's hit me like a piledriver," said Gideon gruffly. "Get all thirty-odd photographs out to all the Press, television, anyone who can use them. If these girls aren't in England it seems to me they're more likely to have been shipped abroad than to have been murdered. Whichever way it is, it's very bad. We want news of any of them—and we want it urgently."

Both men were already getting up from their chairs, and in a few moments they had gone, leaving Gideon in a mood not far removed from tension and alarm.

Thirty-two girls—

He muttered to himself, "What a morning!" and glanced at the reports. The church problem, the gold problem, the photo-nudes problem. A new thought came, relaxing him for the first time since the shock of the silence when he had realized the full significance of what the Superintendents had implied. Religion—money—sex; the three motives which controlled most human behavior now demanded the attention of the Yard more than they ever had before.

Gideon felt a heavy burden of responsibility far beyond one man's due.

If he failed in any one of these investigations, how deep would the effect of such failure be?

CHAPTER 17
BRIEFING

The lecture room at the Yard was neither large nor impressive. It was pleasant to know that when the new building down the river was ready there would be at least two lecture halls for instruction and for briefing. Meanwhile they had to make do with what they had, and that morning, just after half-past eleven, the largest available room was crowded to overflowing with Divisional Superintendents, their chief assistants, the Commander of each of the districts into which the Force was divided, the Commander of the Uniformed Branch, and a few other key officers. As Gideon stepped inside the room, which was already thick with smoke, there was a pause in the hum of conversation. Lemaitre, at a table which stood on a small dais, waved to him.

"Be a bit of a mess if someone blew up this lot, wouldn't it?" He grinned, obviously delighted with himself. "Going to take the chair, George?"

"I can't stay long," Gideon told him.

"Pity," said Lemaitre, trying hard to disguise his pleasure. "I asked Hobbs. He hasn't come in at all yet."

Gideon said, "I know. Are you ready?"

"Yes—I've the plan of campaign."

"Right." Gideon went to the front of the dais, his right hand raised. Silence fell immediately. It was a long time since he had seen so many senior officials together, and by the nature of things, most of those present were in his own age group—the middle forties to the middle fifties. There were at least a dozen with whom he had walked the beat, when superintendency had been a far-off dream. He had a warmth of affection for most of them, and knew that it was returned; but he wondered how many, if any, would have the faintest idea what he was talking about if he attempted to describe to them the overwhelming feeling of responsibility which lay so heavily on him.

They fell silent. Usually he would have been ready with a joke, but this wasn't the morning for any kind of lightheartedness.

"Glad you could all make it," he said in a carrying voice. "But I'm sorry it was necessary. Our biggest worry, as you must have realized, is the church outrages. There *is* a danger that we might think, because we had a quiet time last night, that we're over the worst. I don't believe it for a moment. Whether we like it or not we've got to gear ourselves for a continuing effort until we find out who's behind it. Lemaitre will tell you how we think it can best be done. I want to tell you that it's just about the gravest problem I've ever had to deal with at the Yard."

"And that's saying something," Lemaitre interpolated in a loud aside.

"There's another case in which I need your help," Gideon went on, "but before I mention what it is—do any of you have any ideas about the motivation of the church crimes?"

For a moment no one spoke, but a man with a north country voice suggested from the back of the room, "Religious persecution, maybe."

"Intolerance, I was going to say," put in a Welshman.

"Plain bloody hate," a Cockney piped up.

"Insanity," suggested another.

"There are probably quite a number of these vandals," Gideon remarked. "Madmen don't normally get together and plan a campaign like this. Let's cut out insanity."

"Fanatical hatred of the Church," the Welshman suggested.

Two or three others began to speak at the same time, but stopped when Gideon raised his voice. "All right, so no one has any ideas we haven't tossed around ourselves. When Lemaitre's briefed you, it would be a good idea to have a discussion, something might come out of it. There is one important point to consider, for instance, and that is that instructions for the last crop of outrages must, in all probability, have been sent out the day before the incidents. How? At a meeting like this? By telephone? By letter? By personal messenger? But I needn't elaborate." Gideon paused, until he was sure they all realized he had finished with the church crimes, and then went on. "Now about another matter. We're gravely worried over the photo-nudes." Only two or three men grinned, a clear indication that most of these took the photo-nude murders very seriously. "Golightly and Rollo will see you all get a set of thirty-two photographs. All but the murdered three are missing, without trace. We want any line at all on any one of them. If you get even a whisper of information, send it through to us at once."

There was a murmur of understanding, and several men echoed, "Thirty-*two*."

"Over to you, Lem," Gideon said.

On this kind of assignment, Lemaitre was good; anything that assured him of the limelight and fed his ego also assured his effectiveness. Gideon left him with feet planted firmly, head and shoulders thrust slightly forward in a form of restrained aggressiveness. As he entered his own office the outside telephone bell rang.

"Yes."

"Mrs. Gideon, sir."

At last! "Put her through . . . Hallo, Kate, I've been trying to get you." Gideon infused a little lightheartedness into his voice, which was always easy for him to do with Kate. "Been buying up London?"

"George," Kate said, "did you know Helen Hobbs was in a very bad way?"

Gideon caught his breath.

"No. But I had an idea she was not too good. In fact that's what I was ringing about—to ask you to go and see her."

"She isn't likely to last the day," Kate said quietly.

Again Gideon caught his breath, and this time it hurt. Kate would not say such a thing unless she had been sure.

"I've just been there," Kate told him. "Alec was with her."

"Oh," said Gideon. "He—I hope he doesn't feel he must come into the office."

"He does. He wants to."

"He mustn't. He—"

"George," interrupted Kate, "he can't do any good. She's in a coma, and the doctors say there's no chance that she will come out of it. That's what I wanted to ask you. Is there something he can really concentrate on?"

The church outrages—the gold—the photo-nudes.

"Dozens," Gideon said.

"He mustn't have time to think."

"I know."

"George," Kate said with a sob in her voice, "she still looks so beautiful."

Alec Hobbs stood with his back to the window, studying his wife's face. In the coma she looked peaceful, as if she were indeed asleep. Although the illness had wasted her body, it had never touched her face; thin she was, but not gaunt. She still had some color, and her beautiful black hair shone with its early luster. She did not appear to be breathing. When she had first been seized with the respiratory onslaught she had been in pain, but there was no pain now. Then, in between spasms, she had liked to be able to look out of the window which overlooked the river which she loved. Now her bed was raised at the head, so that the reflection which played about Gideon's face and hands, only a mile along the river, played on the eyes which were closed forever.

Hobbs had stood there for a long time.

Slowly he moved and turned his back on his wife, looking out onto the river's sparkling bosom, seeing tugs and barges and some pleasure craft, trivial against the might of the Battersea Power Station. He had come home and found her sitting here so often, so patiently, and love for her and grief for her had had to be lightened to a gentle gaiety. Now all that was over.

He turned away, unable to face the ebbing of her life.

In the next room, a middle-aged nurse put down a magazine.

"I'm going to the Yard," Hobbs said. "You can get in touch with me there."

"Certainly, sir."

He nodded and went out, turned left along Chelsea Reach

and walked stoically, agony held off a handsbreadth away, toward Westminster and Scotland Yard. Passing a new church close to the Embankment, which served a host of flats and houses built on the sites of others destroyed by bombing two or more decades ago, he thought of the outrages; then he noticed a uniformed constable. He paused.

"Keeping an eye open?" he asked.

"Yes, sir." The man drew himself up almost to attention. "We're being *very* careful here, sir. There's a lot of gold in some of the altar plate and the candlesticks and chalices— very valuable, as well as sacred." The officer was an earnest man of middle age.

"What's the cooperation like?"

"Excellent, sir. Couldn't be better. There are at least four church members on duty there day *and* night. Not much chance of trouble here, I'm glad to say."

"Good," Hobbs said. "Keep your eyes open." He walked on.

A spasm of pain shot through him. Keep your eyes open, open, open, open—but Helen's eyes were closed. Eyes open, keep them open—my God, wouldn't he like to catch the devils who were doing this. If only Lemaitre had some other job—

The leader of the "devils" who was organizing the outrages on the churches sat at his desk, brooding over the great tower of the Cathedral. In front of him were the daily papers with their varying stories about what was being done to save the churches. Each gave it the main front-page headline as well as a continuation inside, and each newspaper carried an editorial. The tabloid *Daily View* said:

It is quite incomprehensible that any man or woman, or group of men or women, should set out to commit not only crime but sacrilege. We do not believe that any crime committed in London—in fact in the whole of the British Commonwealth—has ever shocked the public so deeply. Nor do we believe that the conscience of the British people has ever been stirred so much as it has been by this abominable campaign of destruction.

It is conceivable, we believe, that good can come out of even so great an evil as this. The people *are* stirred— and perhaps this will awaken them to an awareness of their own shortcomings. Never has church membership been at so low an ebb. If these crimes should give birth to a great revival in religion, who can deny that good will once again triumph over evil?

Already, there are signs that this may be happening. Hosts of ordinary people, our fellow men, are forming vigilante committees, as it were, to guard their churches, the places where they worship. Such spontaneous action is admirable. The only danger is that in their determination to stop the outrages, the authorities might overlook the first essential—which is to find the evil men who are committing these crimes against God and Man.

The more popular *Globe* said:

The public is shocked, and the public conscience is shocked. These are good things. So is the immediate reaction of the police and the official bodies of the church, in preparing and carrying out a plan of defense. Time may have been lost in the past; none is being lost now.

No outrage was committed last night, but this must not persuade anyone concerned to relax their vigilance for a single moment. Until the perpetrators of the outrages are caught, no church can be safe.

And when we say this we are fully aware that we can envisage danger to our great historic churches and cathedrals, part of the British as well as the Christian heritage. Imagine the cry of horror that would rise if the ancient Coronation Chair were damaged at Westminster Abbey; or the portions of the Bayeux Tapestry were burned. The bones of Edward the Confessor, the Abbey's founder, would lie uneasily indeed.

Or imagine the fine mosaic decorations of the ceilings of the Choir at St. Paul's being ruined; or the noise which would reverberate round the world if there were an explosion in the whispering gallery in St. Christopher Wren's noble edifice.

The danger to these, and to every sacred building in the nation, will remain until the criminals are caught.

The organizer of those criminals read through these and other editorials until he had as clear a picture as a man could have of the defenses and forces ranged against him. He showed no triumph, no egotistical delight at being the root and cause of nationwide attention. Indeed, there were minutes when his face seemed so still that it was hard to see whether he was breathing.

Presently he put all the papers aside and placed his elbows on the desk, the tips of his fingers together in an attitude almost of prayer. No one could deny that he had the face of an ascetic, even if the expression was touched with a chilling arrogance. No warmth, no troubled doubt emanated from him, and in this statuesque pose he stayed for some time. When eventually he broke it, it was with a sharp intake of breath, which heralded a change in his manner. He became alert and quick-moving. Animation returned to his face, expression to his eyes. He lifted a telephone, dialed, and when he was answered said crisply, "I wish to see the Committee of Three in half an hour."

A man said, with the quietness of humility, "We shall be here, sir."

CHAPTER 18
THE COMMITTEE OF THREE

The man who had telephoned the curt message was Hector Marriott, who described himself as a Professor of Languages and who as such had once given private tuition. That was some time ago, before he had inherited his father's money. He was in fact a millionaire, although few were aware of it; so many of his stocks were managed by trusts, so many of his properties were owned under different names. He had for many years managed his affairs skillfully and successfully, making more and more money, although its amassing appeared to give him little pleasure. He was an ascetic. He was also a man with a mission. And he was a man who had visions.

A great many men have visions; only those who believe them to be inspired are likely to be dangerous. Marriott was absolutely convinced of that inspiration; he felt that no vision would ever direct him along the wrong path.

For many years he had worshiped in an ordinary Anglican church, a member but not active in his membership or one of whom much notice was taken. Mr. Marriott, it was said, preferred to keep himself to himself. He did not resent this, but it did nothing to endear him to his fellow members.

During the war the church received a direct hit and was utterly destroyed. The parishioners, such as were left at home, built a wooden shack by their own endeavors, made a wooden altar, fashioned a wooden cross, and worshiped there. The simplicity of the place of worship and the friendliness of the people did a thing which was unique in Marriott's experience. Together, they warmed him. He actually began to like people and to stop thinking that all they wanted was his money. He had never known happiness in the true sense of the word—he had never been in love, although he had had the normal, occasional relationships of the average man—but during the wooden hut period he had been nearer to happiness and contentment than ever before. After a while, however, some of the other church members had become restless, wanting something more materially worthy in which to worship, and a rebuilding fund had been launched.

Marriott had subscribed cautiously; he had even agreed to serve on the Rebuilding Fund committee.

Before long, arguments had started. The target crept higher, more and more expense was incurred on gold, on silver, on rich embroideries, on rare woods. Gradually, the fund drove away all thought of worship. There were quarrels. There were jealousies. There were refusals to give to deserving charities. There was even quarreling about ritual.

Hector Marriott resigned, simply, and without verbal protest.

The time came when the new church was built and the first service was held, and in spite of his doubts Marriott had attended. That was the day when, in a church notice, these words, under the name of the vicar, appeared:

"I have good news for all of us, especially for those who have labored so long in preparation for this beautiful new House of God. The site on which our old church stood and where our hut now stands has been sold to very great advantage. We shall now be able to adorn the altar and the pulpit, the choir stalls and the windows, in a way which is worthy of their high purpose."

Hector Marriott, unaware that he was already mad, left the church determined never to set foot in it or in any other so-called place of worship again. Next day, passing the end of the street, he saw a cloud of dust or smoke and went to see what it was. The little hut which he had so loved, not knowing that it was love, was a smoke-filled ruin, the sides split, the roof off, the door torn from its hinges. The demolition contractors on the site simply stated, "It wasn't worth saving —we had to blow it up."

Hatred overflowed in Hector Marriott's heart.

Still not knowing—to his last day not knowing—that he was insane, he had gone home and sunk to his knees, calling upon God to strike down the destroyers. And that night, in his dreams, he had had a vision: that the new church itself should be destroyed in the pride of its idolatry. At first he had believed that the church would destroy itself, that his dream would be fulfilled in that way, but he had other dreams —that he himself should be the instrument of such destruction.

He began to daydream.

He was an ascetic, he hated war, he did not know the love of a woman or love for a woman, he was a psychopath, he had millions of pounds to do what he liked with—but the only desire he felt was to desecrate and eventually destroy what others, in the name of worship, had built up.

How?

He waited for a "vision" and one came: in a dream, he saw himsef and other men standing amid the smoke-rimmed debris of a church. So he must not do this alone. He did not feel any sense of urgency, simply one of purpose; and so he studied books and records of other religious rebels, especially those who had rebelled against the pomp and ceremony of the church, from Luther to Billy Graham, across the centuries and across the world. A study of strange and out-of-the-way religions began to fascinate him, and he went to services of little-known sects, even crossing the Atlantic in his search for information that would nourish his vision.

There he found the sex sects, the worshipers of Baal and of Osiris. He found the Doukhobors who wrestled—as he wrestled—with the spirit, so as to purify its doctrines, and who flagellated themselves and each other in their lust for purification. He felt drawn toward the Shakers in their belief in a celibacy which would destroy themselves, toward the Amanas who had the same horror of sex. He was revolted by the cult of voodoo, half Christian, half black magic, with its awful rituals and terrifying superstitions. He visited the hills of Tennessee where the snake worshipers prayed in the name of Christ; he traversed the high mountains of Utah into the hinterland where some still practiced polygamy, convinced it was the will of God because the Prophet, Joseph Smith, had seen a vision—as he, Hector Marriott, had seen visions.

But *his* were true.

In the course of these travels and meetings he found other men who had the same ascetic tendencies as himself, the same resentment toward the wealth of the churches, the finery, the jewelry, the *objets d'art*. In time he found himself their leader, for he possessed those two great things which move mountains—wealth and faith in his destiny.

Their sect evolved slowly. A chance phrase which Marriott himself used led to their adoption of the name, The Simple

Brethren. The main difference between them and other Christian sects was the fact that they were a secret society, and that they were all pledged to desecrate and destroy idolatry, pomp and show, and all but the simplest of altars and buildings. In the beginning, the word "destroy" was not used literally, although in Marriott's mind there was always a vision of the ultimate destruction he and others were to bring about one day—and for that day he felt an inexorable lust and yearning. But there was no hurry, no sense of urgency; the time must be ripe, and the perpetrators prepared.

The membership of The Simple Brethren was strictly controlled. Before one could become an associate, papers of extreme erudition in matters of idolatry and rare and strange religions had to be read and approved. Cromwell became a hero, almost a god-head. All Christian sects that worshiped with an absolute minimum of ritual won approval, but none of this was enough. Marriott and his closer associates began to practice more and more rigorous forms of asceticism and self denial. They had fast days, days of silence, days of flagellation, days of penitence. More and more was demanded of them. They eschewed the pleasures of life almost entirely, even the pleasures of eating and drinking. They denied themselves all forms of sexual indulgence. They eschewed theaters, cinemas, all games, all activities but those of earning their daily living and of worshiping.

Those who were married left their wives and families, though not without support; for Hector Marriott supplied each family's needs, except those for the husband and the father.

Those who had been engaged to marry broke their engagements.

There was no love but their love for one another and, they said and believed, the love of God.

Gradually, the weaker Brethren dropped out of the circle. Only those who could withstand the rigor of such self-discipline and such abnegation before the Lord and before themselves stayed. Over the years there were nearly five hundred who quit for one reason or another, but a hundred and two remained. Now and again a new Brother was admitted to the sect, and there were times when some, deeply awed by Marriott, saw him as the Father of the movement.

To designate him Father Marriott was too reminiscent of the Roman Catholic Church, so they called him Elder Brother.

These were strange men, each clever and competent in his way, each with his own particular gifts, each with the deep conviction that the worship of God should be in the simplest form and in the barest of houses, that the heirlooms of the churches were gifts from the Devil, and that all outward signs of wealth, all insignia, all holy objects which were bejeweled, or of gold, should be destroyed. They saw the church as an enemy of God, and they believed that the enemies of God should be utterly annihilated.

Slowly, painfully, Marriott the Elder Brother trained these men, converting them to his own beliefs, his own visions, almost to believe in his own divinity. They did not worship him but they worshiped through him, and so they worshiped through his madness, becoming one with it.

He had taken to himself three advisers: these were the Committee of Three. But it was Marriott who made the decisions, and he had timed the explosions to coincide with the tenth anniversary of the destruction of the little wooden shed. And it was he who had decided that on each night of action the number of churches attacked would double that of the previous attack. It was a purely arbitrary decision, and inherent in it was the realization that, once launched, the campaign of destruction must quickly reach crescendo to ensure the maximum amount of damage being done before successful methods were put in train to stop the conspirators.

The Committee of Three met in an office in Victoria Street, only five minutes' walk from Marriott's flat. On the hall staircase there was a painted notice: "The Brothers Bible Society—Third Floor." Marriott owned the building, letting it off in offices. He himself occupied three rooms in all, in which he ran a Bible and tract distributing business with a genuine trade. The Committee met, as always, in a room at the back, quietly and unobserved.

When Marriott arrived, the others were waiting, standing by their places at a round table. One, Joliffe, was tall, lean, melancholy. The second, Abbotsbury, was of medium height, thin, sad-looking. The third, Dennison, was sturdier and actually had a little color in his cheeks.

Each was dressed in clerical gray.

Each stood silent until at last the Elder Brother said, "Amen."

All of them sat down.

"You will have seen the effect of what we have done already," said the Elder Brother. "It has been highly successful, the hand of God aiding our endeavors. It will not be so easy in future, however, and so our preparations must be well-considered. Do we all agree?"

There were three murmurs of assent, sounding as one.

"These houses of idolatry are being closely guarded and as closely searched, but we shall be blessed if we overcome our difficulties and cursed if we fail to rise to the opportunities. As you well know, we contemplated the possibility that the police would aid the churches and so we made our plans. Are we all aware of those plans?"

Again a single murmur of unified assent hummed through the room.

"As we are aware, yesterday I sent to sixteen of our Brethren the directive; each knows which house is to be visited next. None must fail."

Assent greeted him.

"If one is apprehended by the police it is possible that he will betray, wittingly or unwittingly, the existence and the dedicated purpose of The Simple Brethren. Since no one knows where I live, and since this office is unknown except to us, we have nothing to fear."

"Nothing to fear. Nothing to fear. Nothing to fear."

"Nevertheless, we will not come here and we will not meet again until I summon you. I will send the directives out as they become necessary. If our efforts are blessed, none of the Brethren will be detected and we shall strike again the night after tomorrow. If, on the other hand, the forces of evil should assert themselves and we cannot foregather, each of us knows the final task."

"I know."

"I know."

"I know."

"Each of us has sworn to accomplish that task, at the risk of his life."

"Each of us has."

"Each of us has."

"Each of us has."

"I will ask each of you to remind himself of his obligation, and to repeat it, under solemn oath. Brother Joliffe."

The tall, lean man said in a frail but steady voice, "I hereby swear by solemn oath of allegiance to The Simple Brethren and to God that at risk to myself, even unto death, I will destroy the house of idolatry known in this land as the Cathedral of Westminster."

"*Ah-men.*"

"Brother Abbotsbury."

"I hereby swear by solemn oath of allegiance to The Simple Brethren and to God that at risk to myself, even unto death, I will destroy the house of idolatry known in this land as the Synagogue of London."

"*Ah-men.*"

"Brother Dennison."

In a firm, clear voice, the third member of the Committee declared: "I hereby swear by solemn oath of allegiance to The Simple Brethren and to God that at risk to myself, even unto death, I will destroy the house of idolatry known in this land as the Abbey of Westminster."

"*Ah-men.*"

There was a pause, which became prolonged. Tension crept stealthily round the room, to be broken by the voice of the Elder Brother, speaking with the slow and frightening clarity of the utterly possessed.

"I hereby swear in solemn oath of allegiance to The Simple Brethren and to God that at risk to myself, even unto death, I will destroy the house of idolatry known in this land as St. Paul's Cathedral."

"*Ah-men.*"

"*Ah-men.*"

"*Ah-men.*"

CHAPTER 19
HOBBS V. LEMAITRE

"Everyone thought the same," said Lemaitre to Gideon. "They all think we're dealing with a lot of cranks and crackpots. Ordinary methods won't do any good, we've got to out-think a bunch of weirdies. What a hope!"

In a quiet voice, Alec Hobbs asked, "You don't view our chances very favorably then?"

"I view our chances of stopping most of the baskets very favorably indeed, but not of finding out who they are," Lemaitre said. He was still a little awkward in Hobbs's company, and rather dogmatic. He did not know about Hobb's wife but he could see the glassy-eyed look and the evidence of strain in the other's manner, and he wondered what it was all about. When Hobbs gave no answer, Lemaitre took silence for implied criticism and went on almost stridently,

"If they have another go tonight at several churches we ought to catch one or two of them, and *if* we can make them talk, then bob's your uncle."

"Don't you think we can make them talk?" asked Hobbs.

Again, Lemaitre took this to imply criticism: *you* can't, *I* can, but not in so many words. He became wary, even more conscious of his position. He was still Hobb's equal in rank but the official promotion to Deputy Commander was due in a matter of days; from then on Hobbs's superiority would be established. Lemaitre thought, if this so-and-so expects me to call him "sir," he's got another think coming.

"I've been at this game a long time," Lemaitre said, picking his words very carefully. "The most difficult ones are the fanatics, the I'll-die-for-a-cause type. If we're dealing with that type, none of us will make 'em talk. Not even the Gestapo could make 'em. You'll see."

"Probably," Hobbs conceded.

They were in his office, across the passage from Lemaitre's and Gideon's, with a view of the courtyard, the parked cars, and a corner of Cannon Row Police Station. It was a small, carpeted office, with a photograph of Hobbs's wife on top of a bookcase and a clock over the mantelpiece. There were no pictures—although the C.I.D. chart showing the "family tree" of the Department, from the Commissioner and Assistant Commissioner down, was centered on one wall. There was more than a touch of austerity, and nothing about the room, excepting the one photograph, was homely or personal.

Lemaitre drew a deep breath. "You got any ideas?" he demanded.

"Not at the moment," Hobbs said. "If anything occurs to me, I'll have a word with you."

"Do that." Lemaitre put a hand on the door. "I'll be out most of the afternoon. Going over to West Central, then up into the City. Gee-Gee's worried about the Abbey and St. Paul's." He opened the coor. "See you," he said, and stepped out.

He stood in the wide corridor for several seconds, watched curiously by a constable on duty in the hall and noticed by several inspectors and detective sergeants who passed. At last he went across to his own office and sat down. On his desk was a note: "Look in, Lem. —G." For once, Lemaitre did not jump to a virtual command but stood at the window, glooming. He was becoming more and more worried about the undertone of criticism or disapproval that he sensed in Hobbs.

"Be a bloody sight better if he'd come straight out with it and say he thinks I'm a clot," he muttered.

There was more to his mood than that. He knew that he was doing everything within his capacity on the church job, but he was beginning to feel out of his depth. He had a sense of impending crisis, a presentiment of danger. When he said that you could not make fanatics talk he knew what he was talking about, and the alarming growth of the sacrilege, the extremes to which its perpetrators were prepared to go, had all the indications of the worst kind of fanaticism. On the crest of a wave of optimism and achievement that morning, when the Divisional Superintendents had dispersed and he was on his own, Lemaitre now felt thoroughly depressed.

Hobbs hadn't helped.

Hobbs never would. The fear of what would happen once he was a superior officer was deep in Lemaitre's mind.

"Better retire early, I suppose," he muttered.

There was a tap at the door. He spun round, as Golightly looked in.

"Where's Gee-Gee, Lem?"

"Isn't he in his office?"

"No. I want a word before I finally pull Entwhistle in."

"Well, I don't know where the great man is."

"Hobbs says go ahead without Gee-Gee. What do you think?"

Lemaitre muttered, "Won't do any harm. If you ask me, Entwhistle ought to have been charged a couple of days ago. Any special hurry?"

"We had a tip-off that he's planning to leave the country."

"Go get him, then," said Lemaitre.

Golightly, obviously satisfied, went out. Lemaitre tapped perfunctorily on Gideon's communicating door and looked in: the office was empty. He fingered the "Look-in" note, said *sotto voce*, "It couldn't have been very serious," wrote across the note "Back six-ish" in his fine copperplate hand, and went out.

Soon he was talking to church officials at St. Paul's and the Superintendent-in-charge from the City Police, checking the security plans. North and West doors, all the chapels, all the altars, the pulpit, the font, the Whispering Gallery and the crypt where so many had worshiped were under constant supervision. His spirits rose. He left in better heart and reached Westminster Abbey, where he found the Superintendent from the Westminster Division. They made a slow, comprehensive tour, mingling unnoticed with parties of sightseers and their guides. Starting at the north entrance, they moved along the Statesmen's Aisle, across to the south transept, passing the High Altar, with its magnificent mosaic of the Last Supper and the great carved stone screen. Wherever there was a thing of beauty or of antiquity, there were people, English and American, German and Japanese, travelers from all over the world, their guidebooks open, their cameras swinging. Past the poppy-framed tomb of the Unknown Warrior, past the memorial to Winston Churchill, beneath the great west window with its warrior figures, Lemaitre and his little party trod their vigilant way.

The farther they went, the more troubled Lemaitre became.

"It's going to be a heck of a job," he remarked.

"We understand that, Superintendent," said the gentle-voiced official with him, "but *every* spot is watched. We have a constant patrol going over the exact route we have taken, day and night. And we have watchers in the galleries, two men in the Henry VII chapel, two at St. Edward's Shrine, four in the nave and the choir stalls. We also have a man in the Muniment Room and two in the Triforium Gallery. The watchers are in the guise of tourists, but each can be identified by the guide book he carries in his right hand—the only one with a green cover."

Lemaitre said to the Divisional man, "And our chaps?"

"Eight dotted about inside, two at the north and west entrances. It couldn't be covered more fully."

Lemaitre forced himself to give a satisfied and congratulatory smile. "Good. That'll foil the beggars."

He thought: one stick of dynamite could do a hell of a lot of damage, though. My God, I wish I hadn't taken this job on.

It was twenty minutes to six when he left the Abbey, walked across to the Houses of Parliament and then along to the Yard.

At twenty minutes to six, Chief Superintendent Percy Golightly looked into the face of Geoffrey Entwhistle and said with great precision:

"It is my duty to charge you with the willful murder of your wife, Margaret Entwhistle, and to warn you that anything you say may be taken down and later used in evidence."

Entwhistle said bitterly, "Okay, use it."

The sergeant with Golightly wrote swiftly in his shorthand notebook.

"What do you mean?" Golightly demanded.

"Use what I saw. I didn't kill her."

"That will be recorded."

"I don't know who did kill her."

"That will be recorded."

"There's a man wandering around London, laughing like hell at you and at me. *He* killed her."

"Your remark will be recorded."

"Oh, to hell with you," rasped Entwhistle. "Let's get going."

"You are at liberty at any time to call your solicitor," Golightly said.

As Entwhistle stepped into the police car which was to take him to Cannon Row Police Station, where he would spend the night before appearing in court next morning, Eric Greenwood walked briskly along Lower Thames Street. He passed the Custom House and Billingsgate Market, where only a few porters, wearing their solid topped hats and their striped aprons, worked on opening crates of frozen fish. He noticed the blueness of their hands, the harshness of their voices as their mallets smacked the marble slabs. Greenwood walked on, up a steep cobbled hill, to an odd-shaped church with threefold steeple. This was the Church of St. James, Garlickhythe. Across the road stood a policeman, who appeared to take no notice of him; but Greenwood was past worrying about policemen, he felt completely safe. He slipped inside the unusually light and lofty church, with its tall columns paneled as high as the gallery. He was looking up at the vaulted ceiling when a man in a dark suit came toward him.

"Good evening, sir."

"Good evening."

"Haven't I seen you here before?"

"I've certainly been here before—to the lunchtime service, usually."

"And in the evenings, I believe."

"Yes," said Greenwood. "I like to look in."

"You are very welcome, sir. Do you know anything about the history of the church?"

Greenwood smiled faintly.

"I was here when it was bombed. I used to fire-watch."

"Good gracious! I had no idea. I was overseas at the time."

"I often wished I was," said Greenwood. "I came and had a look most days when the rebuilding was going on."

"I remember, sir."

"It took a long time."

"It did indeed. Excuse me—aren't you Mr. Greenwood? from Cox and Shielding's?"

"That's right," said Greenwood, both pleased and surprised.

"I was a seaman on the British-India line—I saw you come aboard occasionally."

"It's a small world."

"It is indeed. Mr. Greenwood, I wonder if you could help us?"

"If it's possible, of course I will. What's the trouble?"

"We have some difficulty in the city in getting the evening volunteers we need to watch the churches," the other said. "We are trying to establish a rota of fire-watchers again."

"You mean you think St. James might be attacked?"

"There is no way of making sure," said the verger. "The police have warned us of the danger, and so have the church authorities. The police are giving us as much help as possible but they can't neglect their ordinary duties, can they?"

"I suppose not," said Greenwood. For the first time since entering the church he remembered the policeman he had seen outside St. Ludd's; and he thought of Margaret. "It'd be dreadful if this place were damaged again," he went on.

"It would indeed," agreed the verger. "*Can* you help?"

"I'll be glad to," promised Greenwood. His heart swelled with a sense of righteousness he had not known for a long time. "What are the hours?"

"If you will come along with me to the vestry, sir, I will show you the rota as far as we have completed it. We have all the help we need by day, thanks to the quick response, but between six o'clock in the evening and six in the morning we are in *very* great need."

"I wouldn't mind one night, right through," said Greenwood. "With time off for meals, of course."

The verger's eyes lit up, and the warmth of his thanks made Eric Greenwood, murderer of his mistress, feel a very fine fellow.

"I don't know, dear," Mrs. Dalby said. "I really can't imagine where she's gone. She's very naughty, isn't she?"

Dalby said in a taut voice, "Yes, very."

"It's such a worry, isn't it?"

"Yes, a great worry."

"How long has she been gone now?"

"Six days," Dalby answered.

"That's too long, isn't it?"

"Much too long."

"Dear," said Mrs. Dalby vaguely, her voice still sweet, her smile untroubled, "you don't think anything could have happened to her, do you?"

"I should hope not, Sarah."

"I've been thinking."

"Have you, then."

"Yes, dear. You know that policeman who came to see you this morning."

"I know."

"Why don't you ask him if *he* can find Sally?"

Dalby nearly choked as he turned away from her.

"That's a very good idea, Sarah," he said. "I'll do that."

"I thought perhaps you would," said Sarah Dalby with satisfaction.

As they talked in their strange and unreal way, their daughter lay in the huge double bed, surrounded by mirrors, possessed by a strange tempest of desire which the man with her could not satisfy. This was one of the moods in which she had no fear, no sense of shame or decency, no thought of home.

In the cellar, two stories below, were the photographs of thirty-two girls, twenty-nine missing and three known to be dead.

CHAPTER 20
NIGHT OF ALARM

Gideon thought he heard a movement in Lemaitre's room and opened the door. Lemaitre had just come in from the passage, and for a moment both men stood with fingers on the handle. Gideon saw at once that Lemaitre was worried, but he made no comment. This hour of the day was one for relaxation and as far as possible they would take advantage of it.

"Come in and have a whisky, Lem."

"Oh, thanks. Don't mind if I do."

"Did you know Entwhistle is across at Cannon Row?"

"Denying it right and left," Lemaitre said.

"He was bound to." Gideon went to a cupboard in his desk and took out a bottle, two glasses, and a siphon of soda water. "Have you heard about Hobbs?"

Lemaitre's lips tightened. He gulped down half his drink and stared at the glass, avoiding Gideon's eye.

"What about him?"

"His wife died this afternoon. She'd been in a coma for several days."

Lemaitre, startled almost beyond belief, jerked his head

and his glass up, spilling whisky over his hand. He did not appear to notice it. He stared, unseeing, at Gideon, who was gazing out of the window at the dark clouds behind which the sun was slowly sinking.

"*Dead,*" breathed Lemaitre. "*Dying* for *days?*"

"Yes."

"And he didn't say a word to us—to *me*—about it."

"He didn't tell me until he had to. Kate found out and I heard about it from her."

"Good God. What does he have for a heart?"

Gideon said heavily, "Is that how it affects you, Lem?"

"He certainly doesn't wear it on his sleeve."

"Is he any the worse for that?"

"I see what you mean," muttered Lemaitre. "My God, if anything happened to Chloe—or if anything happened to Kate—we'd be off our heads."

"Think I would wear my heart on my sleeve?" Gideon asked.

Lemaitre said, "I'd be able to see it, anyhow. The poor sod."

Gideon glanced out of the window.

"And I nearly let fly at him this afternoon," Lemaitre went on. "I thought he was being Mr. Flicking Hobbs, Deputy Commander before his time." Lemaitre began to walk about the office. "Never talked about her, did he? I only saw her once, in that wheel chair—most beautiful woman I've ever seen. Been paralyzed most of their married life, I remember Kate telling me. Cor blinking strewth. I *am* sorry. I really am, George."

"We all are."

"Am I glad I didn't let rip!"

"Why did you come so near it?"

"He was being supercilious, as I thought—hinting at things without coming out into the open. I began to wonder what the hell it would be like when he was officially promoted."

Gideon looked back from the river. Lemaitre finished his drink and Gideon waved to the bottle, in a silent "help yourself." Lemaitre did so, drank again, moving restlessly as if he could not meet Gideon's gaze.

"Lem, I have to go to Paris for two or three days, starting on Sunday night," Gideon told him. "There's a police conference over drugs, and the Customs and Excise people will be there, too. I've been out, checking." In fact he had talked to the Governor of the Bank of England at the club and was convinced of the man's anxiety and insistence on secrecy. "Scott-Marle is bringing Hobbs's promotion forward a couple of weeks, so he will be in charge while I'm gone. It will be a good opportunity for him to find his feet, although a lot of things will be strange to him. They won't be to you."

Lemaitre stopped pacing, and stared.

"I get you," he said.

"I know you do."

"Don't worry, George."

"I'm worried only about one thing."

"What's that?"

"That you won't talk to Hobbs about any problems as freely as you would to me."

Lemaitre drew in a deep breath. "Hobbs will be your deputy, you know, which means a second best, only a second best." He tossed the last of the whisky down. "But you can trust us not to come to blows." He stretched his arms dramatically. "Well, I want to visit half a dozen more churches tonight, George. I was saying to Hobbs, these people are cranks and even if we catch some they won't talk." When Gideon didn't answer, Lemaitre forced a smile and went on. "Here I go, jumping to conclusions again. You mark my words, though. They won't talk." He went to the communicating door. "I'll see you. Er—think there'll be trouble tonight?"

Gideon shrugged. "I hope not. Any idea how our P.C. Davies is?"

"Off the danger list," Lemaitre said. "I looked in at the hospital. No doubt of the blindness, though. What a hell of a thing to happen in a church!"

London was shrouded in lowering skies and battered by a squally wind which made church-watching a more than usually unpleasant duty. All over London the police and the volunteers were alert, from the heart of Mayfair and from Westminster to the slums of the East End, from the sprawling suburbs with their houses cheek by jowl to the residential areas where houses stood in their own grounds; from Camberwell to London Bridge, from Trafalgar Square to Hounslow Heath, from Oxford Circus to St. John's Wood, to Hampstead and beyond, from St. Paul's and the city to Whitechapel and Wapping, Bethnal Green to Rotherhithe—the police stood shoulder to shoulder with Christians and believers as they watched over their churches, some built at the time of the Norman Conquest, some built in the last few years.

The sages shook their heads. "There won't be any trouble tonight. The weather's too bad."

At the synagogue in Marylebone a careful watch was kept

on the ark, and a policeman paced his beat, never out of sight
of the watchers at the entrance for more than ten minutes.
The precautions came easily to those who had long been in
danger of vandalism and to whom the methods of defense
were second nature. None of the watchers seriously expected
trouble, for they did not really believe it would come from
members of their own faith, and surely no gentile could get in
by night.

When a small car turned into the street everyone was
aware of it—even the police constable, who had just passed
the synagogue and heard the car behind him. As he turned
it slowed down and, a moment later, stopped. At once the
policeman's steps quickened. A man got out of the car as
a gust of wind swept along the street at almost gale force.
Rain spattered over the car and its windscreen, shimmering in
the light of the street lamps. Presently the car moved off,
leaving the man behind. The policeman slackened his pace
while continuing to advance.

The watcher at the door spoke mildly. "Can I help you,
sir?"

"Yes." The voice was authoritative. "I have a message for
Rabbi Perlutt."

"He is inside," the watcher said.

"Can I see him, please?"

"I'm afraid you'll have to give me a little more information, sir."

The stranger said, "I have come to warn him."

The policeman, now very close, caught the last words, and
the watcher's echo: "*Warn* him? What about?"

"I am here to tell him that before the sun rises there will be
an attack on your house of worship," the stranger declared,
and he looked up into the face of the policeman. "Did you
hear that, constable?"

"I did, sir. Have you warned Scotland Yard?"

"No, I have not," the man said. "I will give details only to
the Rabbi."

"As a police officer, sir—"

"I am prepared to give a message of great importance to
the Rabbi," the stranger said impatiently. "If he wishes to in-
form the police, that is entirely his affair." He stood still and
aloof, as doubt chased suspicion across the policeman's face.

"I think, sir," said the watcher, "that you should come in.
Please be careful to observe silence, and remember to keep
your head covered. Constable, if you will be good enough to
stay by the door in case the Rabbi wishes to speak to you, I
will be very grateful."

"I'll be here, sir," the constable assured him.

The other led the way to the big hall, in which stood the
ark, the marriage canopy some distance in front of it, and the
reader's desk. There were only a few lights showing, and the
empty spaces seemed full of menace.

As they stepped forward, the stranger put his hand to his
pocket, took out an egg-shaped object, and hurled it at the
ark. As it struck it exploded in a violent yellow flash. A fierce
blast swept along the pews, smashing the windows, blowing
the canopy to smithereens. The policeman heard the roar and
sprang forward, but as he reached the doors the stranger appeared, thrust him aside, and ran into the street. Coming
along was the little car, which slowed down only long enough
for the stranger to scramble inside.

Fire and smoke and awful debris filled the synagogue, and
as men recovered from the shock they raised the alarm which
would bring help.

But the vandal got away.

The same methods were used all over London, against Anglican church and Roman Catholic, some Methodist and one
Presbyterian.

All but two of the destroyers escaped.

Gideon's telephone bell began to ring at dead of night and
he stirred in bed, protesting silently, until he felt Kate move
and was suddenly conscious of the fact that the ringing would
wake her. He stretched out mechanically and put the receiver
to his ear. Still half asleep, he said, "Gideon."

"George, there have been sixteen!" Lemaitre burst out.

Gideon echoed, "Sixteen? Sixteen what?" As soon as the
question was uttered he realized the absurdity of it, but Lemaitre cried, "Sixteen outrages! *Sixteen churches damaged!*"

Gideon could sense the anguish in the other's voice. He
could tell from Kate's stillness that she was awake, but perhaps not fully, yet. He pushed the bedclothes back, whispering
tersely into the receiver, "I'll come over. Any of them
caught?"

"Only two."

Gideon's heart leapt. "We've got two?"

"Yes. They're on their way to the Yard."

"Where are you?"

"At West Central."

"Meet me at the Yard." Then a fearful thought flashed
through Gideon's mind, and he asked sharply, "Any cathedrals damaged?"

"They got the altar at St. Martins in the Furrows," Lemaitre said. "That's the biggest. Er—think I ought to tell Hobbs?"

"No."

"So long as you agree," said Lemaitre.

Gideon got out of bed and flicked on a light faint enough not to disturb Kate. He began to dress, seeing from the illuminated dial of the bedside clock that it was twenty minutes to two. Well, he'd had two hours' sleep.

"Is it serious?" Kate asked, suddenly.

"Nothing desperate yet. Just some more church damage."

"It's wicked," Kate said.

"Downright evil," Gideon agreed. "You stop worrying about it."

"How many were damaged?"

"Sixteen."

"*Sixteen.* Why, that's twice as many as the last time!"

"They seem to be doubling after each outrage," Gideon remarked. "Don't worry about me if I don't come back. I'll probably bed down at the Yard."

In fact he was not likely to get any more sleep tonight. As he made his way to the garage through the chill of a now dry but blustery morning, he yawned and was aware of being tired; he needed more sleep than he used to. No—he needed to sleep more regularly, he could not throw off the effect of late or broken nights as easily as he had done when younger. But what did it matter? He drove along the Embankment, passed Millbank House, and saw the vague outline of Lambeth Palace across the river. At least eight uniformed policemen were in sight of St. Margaret's Church and the Abbey. What a thing to come to pass—the churches, guarded by the law! They would have to call the military out if the situation got much worse, and so history would repeat itself. He turned into the Yard, and found more than the usual bustle. Up in the C.I.D. offices lights blazed, men walked and talked noisily, there was a great wave of activity. He opened Lemaitre's door, but the room was empty, went into his own room and found the lights on, coffee on a tray, all the signs that it had been used within the past few minutes. Smoke rose straight from the stub of a cigarette in the ashtray. Lemaitre didn't smoke cigarettes these days. He was at the door when it opened and Scott-Marle appeared, gaunt and aloof.

"Hallo, sir!"

"Hallo, Commander." The Commissioner was always formal when others were present, and Lemaitre and another

Chief Superintendent were just behind him. "I want you to interrogate the two prisoners yourself."

"I will, sir."

"I've asked Lemaitre to prepare a detailed plan of the locations of tonight's outrages, and to assess the total extent of the damage."

"I'll get on to it at once, sir," Lemaitre promised.

"Thank you."

"One thing," Gideon said. "Has anyone been hurt tonight?"

"Not seriously," Lemaitre said. "That's one relief, anyhow. A few cuts and bruises. One of the so-and-so's has damaged his arm pretty badly, he's the worst as far as I know." He glanced at Scott-Marle. "I'll get down to the plan, sir." He hurried into his office, then bobbed back: "They're over at Cannon Row, Geo—Commander."

The door closed on him.

Gideon looked at the other Chief Superintendent and said, "Bring the two prisoners up and stay with them in Mr. Hobbs's room until I send for them." When the man had gone he studied Scott-Marle's drawn and troubled face, and went on. "Do you wish to be present at the interrogation, sir?"

"Do you think it would be wise?"

Gideon hesitated, deliberating the matter, then answered with a diffidence that barely sounded in his voice, "No, sir."

"Very well," Scott-Marle said. "I will be in my office. Don't rush the interrogation on my account, Commander."

CHAPTER 21
CANNON ROW

In Cannon Row Police Station, awaiting the Magistrate's Court hearing of the charge, was Geoffrey Entwhistle, pale and haggard and unshaven, feeling weak and helpless one moment, enraged the next. During the past week he had relied on whisky to keep up his morale, and he had not had a drink for hours. He sat on the narrow bed, head in his hands, hardly able to believe that such a thing had happened to him. He had not yet named a solicitor because, so far, he had had very little need of one. At the same time he felt the situation to be so hopeless that to fight it would be a waste of effort. They had him; they would convict him.

Suddenly, he jumped up and cried, "And they won't even hang me!"

The police sergeant on duty in the cells heard him, went along, listened, heard a repetition, and noted it down.

Two cells along the corridor, out of earshot, was one of the two men caught raiding a church. He was short, compact, in his late forties, clean-shaven, rather austere-looking. He had refused to give his name. He had been searched but nothing in his pockets or on his clothes gave any clue to his identity. Next to him was another man, taller, equally silent, equally good-mannered. Next to this tall man was the thief whom Eric Greenwood had disturbed at St. Ludd's. He was here because the second hearing was due early the next morning, and Lemaitre wanted to question him again and make quite sure he was not connected with the vandalism.

This man was sleeping.

In other cells there were two prostitutes and a woman who had tried to kill herself and her illegitimate infant. A welfare officer was with her, soothing the hysteria of despair.

A plain-clothes sergeant came hurrying down from the station above.

"The two men are wanted," he said. "Have they shown any sign of violence?"

"Mild as milk," the sergeant answered, and then two more officers came, each carrying handcuffs. "You won't need those," the sergeant declared.

"We aren't taking any chances."

The two vandals were removed from the cells without fuss, handcuffed, and taken up to the Yard. Four uniformed and two more plain-clothes men were there. A photographer at the gates let out a yell and rushed forward into the forbidden territory of the Yard, his light flashing. Two officers closed on him. The contingent of big men, towering above the prisoners and watched by dozens of night-duty men and Flying Squad officers, went in the back way and up in the big, iron-gated lift. At the first-floor level three men stood waiting.

Throughout all this, the two prisoners had not changed their expression or uttered a word. Now, with a guard in front and one behind, they were taken to Hobbs's office and escorted inside. They were kept waiting for five minutes before a sergeant came in.

"The first accused, please," he said.

There was a moment's hesitation before the taller of the two men stepped forward. As he crossed the passage, he saw the door with the name COMMANDER GIDEON. One man tapped on this door and then opened it.

Gideon stood with his back to the window. The prisoner stepped inside.

"Take off the handcuffs," Gideon ordered. "And wait outside."

Gideon had become a student of men the hard way, from the bitter experience of trial and error, of betrayed trust, of honesty and dishonesty concealed by the most unlikely faces. He studied this prisoner as closely as he had ever studied anyone. The first impression never left him; the man was an ascetic. The face was lined, but not deeply; the lips were set, but not tightly. His features were clean-cut and his skin had the clearness which some devotees of extreme physical fitness show, an almost aggressive purity. There was no spare flesh on him, no hint of plumpness. He was dressed in a clerical gray suit, well-cut not in any particularly modish way. His graying hair was cut quite short.

Gideon knew that he had not uttered a word since his arrest outside St. Butolph's in the Strand.

Gideon held his own peace for at least two minutes, before saying casually, "Good evening."

The man was surprised into opening his mouth, actually forming the letter "g," and in that moment Gideon felt a flare of triumph: once start him talking and he might go on and on.

But no sound came; the thin lips closed again. Gideon kept silent for a few seconds, and then remarked, "So you've taken a vow of silence."

The reaction was sufficient to convince him that the guess was right. The pale eyes narrowed, a gleam of surprise flickered in them but soon died away. Now Gideon felt no flare of triumph, rather one of dismay. If the prisoner *had* taken a vow of silence he would almost certainly keep it, and what was true of him would probably prove true of any others who were caught. Lemaitre had known what he was talking about.

Gideon said, "Presumably you are aware that you have committed a very grave crime, not only against the church, but against the laws of the country."

There was no answer.

"The maximum penalty for sacrilege is imprisonment for life. Do you realize that?"

The man showed no flicker of interest.

"Life imprisonment is no joke, Mr.——"

There was no response.

"Your wife and family may have plenty to say," remarked Gideon.

No answer.

"You know, all you are doing is wasted effort," Gideon said, as if to himself. "A good try but bound to fail. If you'd simply been seen we might have had trouble in identifying you, but when we put your photograph in the newspapers and on television, someone is bound to come forward and identify you. After that it will be simply a question of routine questioning of your relations, your friends and your acquaintances. Failure to identify you, and through you your associates in these crimes, is out of the question. You haven't a chance."

The man standing so still in front of him did not flicker an eyelid.

Ten minutes later Gideon gave up.

Half an hour later he gave up on the smaller prisoner, too.

Immediately afterward he went across to see Scott-Marle, who was alone in his office, poring over a map of London in which the churches were marked with crosses. He glanced up, hopeful for a moment, then settled back in his chair.

"I'm as nearly sure as I can be that they've taken a vow of silence," Gideon told him. "Both men reacted in exactly the same way to the same questions. I should say they've not only taken a vow but they've also practiced living up to it. And if we catch any more they'll be the same."

Scott-Marle, his eyes very red-rimmed, said gruffly, "You're not often pessimistic."

"I am about making these men talk. But we can have their photographs in tomorrow's—I mean today's—evening papers and on television. By the day after tomorrow we're bound to get some form of identification. From then on we should be on the way to finding who they are and what they're up to, but—I'll be in Paris."

Scott-Marle said, "Yes. You must be."

"And it may be too late," Gideon warned. "These men aren't fools. They know that from today on, their number's up. But they've taken some pretty big risks last night, and they might take bigger ones for bigger objectives."

"Then before you go, make sure everything is tied up so that nothing avoidable can go wrong," Scott-Marle ordered. When Gideon made no comment, he went on with a faint smile, "I know, I'm tired, George." After another pause, he went on. "It's a thousand pities Hobbs can't be on duty. How do you think Lemaitre is going to make out?"

Gideon said with forced confidence, "He's missed nothing so far."

Before Scott-Marle could comment there was a tap at the door, and at Scott-Marle's "come in," Lemaitre entered, carrying a long roll of paper.

"All finished, sir."

"Good. Let me see." There was a high table at one side of the room, rather like a drawing board, and Scott-Marle held the paper flat while Lemaitre, with fingers fluttering with eagerness, pinned them at the corners. There was an outline map of London with every major road marked, and a crisscross of thin lines, like rivers on an ordinary map, showing the minor streets. There were different-colored crosses in a spreading rash over the whole area.

"The black are for Anglican churches, the blue for R.C. . . ." Lemaitre's voice was quick with suppressed pride, the words tumbling over each other. "And the red stars show where we've had the trouble—one star, the first night of attack, two the second, three last night—"

Not wishing to detract from Lemaitre's brief hour of importance Gideon said quietly, "Do you need me any more now, sir?"

"No, Commander. Lemaitre can tell me all I need to know."

Gideon went out and along to his office, pleased for Lemaitre, but deeply worried over the matter as a whole. There was now no shadow of doubt that they had to deal with religious fanatics and should start concentrating on the known off-beat sects. Time was the problem; he had a sense of urgency which Scott-Marle shared, but what serious hope was there of getting this investigation finished quickly? They needed weeks.

He turned into his office and found Rollo by his desk, drawing fiercely at a cigarette. In spite of the pressure of the church crimes Gideon's thoughts flashed immediately to the photo-nudes murders and to the missing girls.

"Heard you were in," Rollo said.

"Got anything?" demanded Gideon.

"I think we know the man—a Toni Bottelli."

"Where is he?"

"Owns a tobacconist and newspaper shop in Tottenham," said Rollo. "He's got a cellar on the same scale as Rhodes's. Often has girls down there to photograph—we've found one of the girls."

"One of those we're looking for?"

"No. One who went down to the cellar and didn't like what she saw," Rollo said. "She came forward because she recognized some of the photographs we've had in the papers. She'd seen the same photos in the cellar before."

Gideon said gruffly, "Thank God for this much. What have you done?"

"Thrown a cordon round the place."

"Not too close, I hope."

"Complete coverage, but it can't arouse suspicions," Rollo assured him. "Look." He picked up a sectional map of North London, drawn on a much larger scale than the one Lemaitre had taken to Scott-Marle, and pointed. "There's the shop—in the High Street. It's halfway along the block. There's a service road behind it, there." The service road was marked clearly. "There's the back of the shop and the living quarters above. Follow?"

"Yes."

"We've men in parked cars in the High Street, and they took up their posts one at a time. We've men in the side streets whom Bottelli can't see." He paused. "We've four men in the service road, covered by garages and outhouses so that they can't be seen either. At a signal they can all converge on the back yard. The service alley can then be sealed off."

"Roof?" Gideon asked.

"There's a roof light. We've also planted a man on the roof at the end buildings of the block."

"What do you plan to do?"

"A straight move in from the front," said Rollo. "Provided Bottelli isn't given any warning, I don't see that he can do much. Golightly's over there, in charge. He agrees with me."

Gideon didn't speak.

"I can't see Bottelli putting up much of a fight," Rollo went on. "It's one thing to play around with a camera and a lot of girls in the altogether, but when he realizes what he's up against, he'll just cave in."

"Sure he's there?" asked Gideon.

"Yes."

"Sure the girl's there?"

"*A* girl's there all right."

"How do you know?"

"I'll tell you," Rollo said, with a funny kind of smile, perhaps one of distaste. "There's a Peeping Tom in a room opposite. A few weeks ago he got an eyeful—he says there's a room of mirrors over Bottelli's shop and he thought he was seeing a nude beauty contest, but he wasn't. There was a man, too, and our Peeping Tom tumbled to the fact that he was seeing what's what. Ever since then, he's watched hopefully. The curtains are usually drawn by day and by night, but they're open occasionally and he's seen a girl in bed in the mirror room today."

Gideon said slowly, "It looks good enough." He paused, but Rollo didn't interrupt. "Better do as you say," he agreed at last, "but take a couple of women officers along, have a doctor handy, and don't take any chances."

"I tell you the swab will give in the moment he realizes that he's up against us," Rollo said.

Gideon thought, I hope you're right. He didn't say it aloud, because it would serve no purpose; and he was sure Rollo would be as thorough as any man in the Force. He and Golightly between them were almost unbeatable, and to adjure them to be careful or to be thorough would be to treat them like children.

He was a little uneasy, but not worried—not to say worried.

Sally was crying.

They were not deep sobs, yet they were in earnest. She was unhappy and afraid, although she did not know why. The reason was simple: she did not yet know that Toni was drugging her, that she was becoming more and more dependent on the drugs and was happy only when she was under their influence. Now she felt as if she were going to die; she had never known such despair. It was an hour or more since Toni had been with her. In one way she longed to see him again; in another, she shrank from it.

Sometimes he hurt her so. Sometimes—

Tears flooded her eyes, stinging them, and her sobbing became louder. She did not hear Toni come in and so did not see his expression, until suddenly he slapped her across the face and rasped, "Be quiet!"

She gasped and shrank back on the pillows.

"Get up and get dressed," he ordered.

She was trembling with pain and fear, and did not move.

"Get a move on!" he shouted at her, and slapped her again. "Get your clothes on, we're going away."

"But—But—But, Toni—"

He snatched the bedclothes off her, grabbed her wrists, and pulled her out of bed, naked but for a bed jacket which barely reached her waist.

"Get dressed!" he roared. "If you don't, I swear I'll leave you dead."

As he spoke, he drew an automatic pistol from his pocket.

CHAPTER 22
THE PISTOL

Sally Dalby saw the gun, squat and ugly in Toni's hand, and she screamed. For a moment she thought he was going to shoot her, then she was afraid that he would strike her with the weapon. She staggered toward a cupboard, pulled open the door, and dragged out her clothes. As she did so there was the sharp ring of a bell.

She gasped, "What's that?"

"Shut up!" Toni kept the gun in his right hand, and motioned to her with his left. "Put the light out."

"What—"

"Put it out!"

She scurried across the room to the door and pushed the switch up as he reached the window. The sudden darkness frightened her still more. Her breathing was labored, and so was his. She heard a rustle of sound, and faint light came into the room; he had pulled the curtains back and was looking out. She could see the outline of his head and shoulders as he pressed close to the window. Suddenly there was another ring, and Sally jumped wildly.

Toni muttered something, but her teeth were chattering and she did not hear him. The curtains were drawn again, and he called, "Put the light on."

Light? What light? What—

"Put the light on!" he screeched at her. She remembered where she was standing and touched the switch. The light, dazzling, showed him nearly halfway across the room, his gun still in his hand. *"Get your clothes on!"* He yelled. "The cops are here."

Cops?

As his face twisted in rage and alarm, she had never been more afraid of him. Suddenly she began to scramble into her clothes, hardly knowing what she was doing. Bra, panties, slacks, sweater—

"Get a move on!" He flung a pair of moccasins at her and she thrust her feet into them.

"What—what do the police want?"

"You, you silly bitch!"

136

"I—I don't know anything, *I* can't help the police."

"Can't you?" he said, sneeringly; and then, his voice suddenly sharpening, "Well, you can help *me*."

"Toni, *how?*"

"You're going to find out. Come on."

He pulled open the door, and as he did so sounds traveled freely up from the passage alongside the side entrance. Banging, hammering, and voices in a demanding medley. Once, a sentence sounded clearly:

"Open in the name of the law."

". . . fools," Toni muttered.

Still holding her, he reached a spot on the landing beneath a hatch, and she saw a ladder against the wall. He drew this forward, and thrust her toward it.

"Go up, quickly."

"No! I can't stand heights, I—"

"Go up!" He gripped her roughly and she began to climb, holding desperately to the side of the ladder. He followed, half lifting, half shoving her whenever she flagged. As her head touched the hatch, he pushed her furiously upward. "Lever that hatch up."

Terrified to defy him, terrified to let go even with one hand, and trembling violently, Sally eased the hatch open. There were thudding noises and heavy blows downstairs. Toni stretched past her, pressing hard as he flung the hatch back. Cold air swirled round them, snatching at Sally's hair.

"Climb out," Toni ordered. She obeyed blindly, scrambling onto a flat section of the roof, then onto a slanting section. Twice she slipped; each time he stopped her from falling back.

Along the side of the roof, overlooking the street, was a narrow ledge. One slip from it would send them crashing to the ground a hundred feet below. Almost paralyzed with terror, teeth chattering, body quivering, Sally edged along it, crouching, hand touching the slates on one side, Toni, behind her, holding her other hand. Through her terror she tried to speak.

"What are you doing this for? What—"

"Shut up and keep going." After a moment, Toni went on. "I've got another shop along here, we—"

As he spoke, a beam of light shot out from a roof on the other side of the street, shining steadily on him and the girl.

Down on the pavement, opposite the tobacconist's shop, a sergeant was talking to Rollo. Above, lights were flashing; inside, Golightly was leading the raid. Rollo, the younger and

more powerful man, was out here to cover any escape. He
heard a man call out with strident urgency, glanced up, and
saw what looked like a moving ball of light, waving about.
Then he realized that it was a beam of light shining on a girl's
head. Once he knew that, he could see that she was crouching
low and that there was the dark figure of a man behind her.
Along the street a policeman called, "Look!"

"See that?" shouted another.

"There's a girl!"

"See that man?"

Rollo thought: now we could be in for trouble. Aloud, he
said to the sergeant, "We need a fire escape and a catching
net—fix it, quick." He stepped farther into the road, put his
hands to his mouth to make a megaphone and bellowed,
"Don't go any farther! Give yourself up!"

The girl's hair was swept back in the fierce wind; from the
ground she looked quite beautiful.

"You haven't a chance!" Rollo bellowed. "Give yourself
up."

He saw a movement without realizing its significance. He
heard a screeching sound which might be coming from the
girl—the next moment he saw a flash and almost simultaneously heard a bullet crack against the window behind him.
The plate glass broke with a roar like an explosion. Apples
and oranges and other fruit rolled about his feet, shifted by
the falling glass. At the same time detectives appeared on the
ledge some distance from the couple. The man with the girl
must have seen them at the same time, for in the high voice
of desperation he cried:

"Don't come any nearer, or I'll push her off!"

Sally was crouching with her mouth open, trying to utter
screams which would not come. This was a nightmare; she
was helpless *in* a nightmare—and yet she knew it was real,
knew that Toni meant what he said. If the men came any
nearer he would push her off. And if she fell, she would die.

Rollo thought: he means it.

There was that sixth sense, or presentiment, an instanta-
neous recognition of a situation which made the difference
between being a good policeman and a brilliant one, being a
good officer or a born leader. This man would push the girl
off if he thought he was about to be attacked. There would be
no reasoning with him. He had acted on impulse, driven by
fear, and he would again. Almost without thinking Rollo
weighed up the situation, knowing that the only hope lay in

speed. He moved a pace, squashing fruit beneath his feet, realizing that the entire pavement and curb were covered with fruit of all kinds.

The girl's only hope lay in the speed with which the police could act.

He stared up, able to pick out the man and the girl clearly. Two or three of the Divisional men came hurrying, and on the instant Rollo thought: it might work. The couple was within easy aiming distance.

"Listen," he said in a whisper. "Get more men, have everyone pick up apples and oranges, anything heavy enough to throw, and let him have it. *Hurry!*" Aloud, he bellowed: *"You up there!"*

"Don't come any nearer or I'll push her over!" Bottelli screamed.

"Let her go, and we'll let you go!"

"You can't fool me. Call your men off! Call 'em off the roof!"

"I tell you we'll let you go if you let her go!" Rollo shouted. He had half a dozen apples in his pockets and more cradled in one arm, and other men were also armed with fruit. In a whisper, he ordered, *"Throw now."* On the "now" a hail of hard and soft fruit hurtled upward, smashing and spattering on the roof, on Sally, on Bottelli. The policemen below grabbed and hurled, grabbed and hurled, in a furious fusillade.

Up on the ledge, Bottelli suddenly felt something soft splash against his cheeks, then something hard strike him on the chin; next a lucky shot struck the hand holding the gun. He snatched his free hand away from Sally to protect his face. The fruit struck her, terrifyingly, and crouching against the attack she sprawled, spread-eagled, against the slipping tiles. Golightly and two others who had climbed onto the roof, realizing their chance, scrambled forward. Held fast in the beams of torches from the opposite houses, Toni Bottelli fired two shots wildly into the street, then watched helplessly as the gun was struck from his hand.

A detective-officer grabbed him.

Ten minutes later Bottelli was being taken off in a Black Maria to the Divisional Station, and the girl, in sobbing hysteria, was being put into an ambulance for the nearest hospital. The policemen, newspapermen, firemen, and the people from the houses nearby heard the tires crunching over the rolling bananas and apples. Rollo, reaction setting in, began to laugh; once he had started, he couldn't stop.

Gideon heard the news at seven-thirty, when he was called by a detective sergeant, on instructions, from the dormitory bed he had slept on since five-thirty. While he showered he listened to a running commentary from the sergeant on what had happened during the night, then shaved with an electric razor—a method he disliked—and drank very hot tea. The funny side of the fusillade of fruit did not occur to him until later, but in a written report from Golightly there was a generous tribute: "But for Rollo's spontaneous action I doubt if we would have saved the girl's life." Gideon went down to his office and put in a call to the Division, to inquire about the girl.

"She's under sedation at the hospital," he was told.

"The prisoner?"

"He'll be charged today, sir. Mr. Rollo said he would report to you by nine o'clock."

"All right," said Gideon.

No reports had come in yet from the night's crimes. There would be the usual crop and he would have to get through them as best he could. The only case he really worried about was the campaign against the churches. It had become an obsession. Subconsciously, he knew, he was fighting against the Paris mission, but he doubted whether he could persuade Scott-Marle to send anyone else in his place—unless he would agree to send Hobbs, which might be a good thing for the new Deputy Commander. Gideon's heart quite leapt at the thought. He was still deliberating whether to ask Scott-Marle when there was a tap at his door and Hobbs came in. Gideon had no time to hide his surprise.

Hobbs smiled faintly. "I'm not a ghost, George."

"Er—no. Sorry. I didn't think. Well anyway, I'm glad to see you."

"So I imagine. It's been a rough night."

Gideon said gently, "Alec, you know how desperately sorry I am about Helen. If there's a thing I can do, it's as good as done. If you need to be busy for a few days with formalities and family affairs, forget the Yard."

Hobbs's smile deepened. There was a quiet humor in it, a touch of irony, perhaps, in the twist of his lips.

"Helen's brother is looking after the formalities, such as they are." He paused. "There *is* something you can do for me." He stopped.

Gideon looked at him steadily, but Hobbs did not go on. Gideon rounded his desk and said quietly, "Did Scott-Marle tell you I have to go to Paris on Sunday night?"

Hobbs looked surprised. "No."

"Well, I have. A hush-hush conference. Would you like to go?"

Hobbs said flatly, "No. But you're on the right track."

"You must keep busy—yes." Gideon brooded. "I think the next two or three days are going to be as busy and as harassing as I've ever known. But I won't be here."

Hobbs didn't speak.

"Alec," Gideon said, "if you're under such severe emotional strain, can you stand the added burden of this as well?"

Hobbs answered quickly, "Yes, I think so. What you can do for me, George, is to let me sit in on all this morning's briefings, so that I can get an indication of all that's going through. Then let me know your ideas about the cases. After that I'd like to plunge in deep."

Without a moment's hesitation Gideon said, "Right. Let's get started." He shifted his chair to one side, Hobbs pulled up another, and Gideon drew the reports to him and began to go through them, one by one. By the time they had finished it was nearly nine o'clock. Hobbs asked few questions and made few notes, but Gideon had no doubt that he had absorbed almost all there was to know about the cases. The arrest of Geoffrey Entwhistle was touched on but not discussed. The quality of Hobbs the detective was not in doubt, and Hobbs the executive officer was as established; but Hobbs the humanitarian—that was still a big question.

He said, "We've only the one great anxiety then: the church crimes."

"Yes," agreed Gideon.

"I'd like to interrogate the two prisoners."

"Go ahead."

"And if they won't say anything to me, I think they should be questioned by different officers, each officer with a different personality and approach. Lemaitre after me, perhaps, then Golightly, then Rollo. They shouldn't be allowed to rest or to take it easy."

Gideon frowned. "No," he said dubiously. "There's no need to have them in court today. Of course, we can keep at them, but they must have a chance to send for a lawyer. We certainly can't overdo the pressure. You know that as well as I do."

"They won't send for a lawyer, for fear it would help us to identify them," Hobbs reasoned. "And you're too sentimental, George. They've got to be made to talk, and we have to bend every rule in the book to make them. *Bend*," repeated Hobbs, looking very steadily at Gideon. "Not break."

Gideon returned the challenging gaze levelly.

"I don't think we're going to get results by subjecting these two men to any particular kind of pressure. I think we've got to increase the effort in other ways." He paused for a long moment and added: "Talk to Lem about it, will you? I think we should concentrate a lot more on out-of-the-way and little-known sects—what might be called the religious lunatic fringe."

"Only don't say that in public," cautioned Hobbs.

That was so characteristic of a remark Gideon himself might make that it was like hearing himself speak. Gideon had not fully recovered when there was a tap at the door, and Lemaitre strode in.

CHAPTER 23
SEARCH FOR SIMPLICITY

Lemaitre was obviously pleased with himself, so much so that even seeing Hobbs did not put him out of his stride. He slapped his hands together loudly, boomed, "Good morning, all!" and then his expression changed ludicrously and he stared open-mouthed at Hobbs.

"What a clot I am," he gasped.

Quickly, quietly, Hobbs said, "Let's take some things as said, Lem." He smiled quite freely. "And I don't mean that you're a clot! The Commander and I have come to the unoriginal conclusion that our only pressing problem is the church outrages. We feel a desperate need for a new approach."

Lemaitre swallowed hard, gave Hobbs a sidelong glance, then rubbed his knuckly hands together. "New or old, what does it matter? I'm onto something."

Gideon felt a surge of excitement, rare in him. Hobbs stiffened.

"I've been following an angle you mentioned earlier, George. Cranky religious sects, and these chaps are cranks if ever I've known one. You know that old boy we saw over at St. Denys's in Kensington?" Gideon recalled the almost skeletal face of the old man in the damaged church, and remembered the girl Elspeth who had come to him, so soothingly. "Well, I happened to know he's a bit of a crank himself, very interested in out-of-the-way religions, made a proper study of it. I happened to notice the books on his shelves. That set me thinking. So I went over to see him the next day, and asked him to make out a list of all the off-beat sects in London—England really, but most of them are in London."

Gideon thought, why didn't he tell me? He said, "Nice work, Lem."

"I'll say it was nice work," Lemaitre crowed. "There are dozens in London, and they range from West Indian voodoo worshipers and Tennessee snake worshipers to the Black Mass boys. We'd find some sun worshipers if we look hard enough, I dare say. And then we were on the lookout for buyers of dynamite, remember?" He did not pause for comment, but careered on. "Funny thing about that dynamite. I couldn't understand it. Why *dynamite?*"

He paused, not for an answer from the others but in a kind of artistic triumph. Hobbs glanced at Gideon, who was watching Lemaitre intently, and thinking: he had to justify himself, that's why he's been keeping all this back. He was astonished that Lemaitre, always bursting to talk, could have been going ahead like this and keeping his own counsel.

"I mean, why not nitro? Or cellulose nitrate? Or any of a dozen things easier to conceal. Why *dynamite?* Because it was easy to get hold of, or because it had some kind of significance? Remember the man Bishop, George? He tried to burn London down because his wife and kids were burned to death in a slum fire."

"I remember." It was like being asked if one remembered the Battle of Britain.

"Anyway, the Vicar of St. Denys's, Kensington—old Miles Chaplin, you saw him—gave me these lists of sects and their leaders, some of them so obscure hardly anybody knows about them. I had every one checked—just as you said—and had a special eye kept open for one of them who could get hold of dynamite easily. *"And,"* brayed Lemaitre, "I found it."

Very softly, Gideon said, "Well done, Lem."

"Sect called The Simple Brethren," Lemaitre said. "*Very* strict, they even think the Quakers are ritualists. Run by a man named Marriott, Hector Marriott. They call him the Elder Brother. He's got pots of money, and owns a lot of businesses, and—here's the significant fact—one of them is for the manufacture of fireworks!"

"My God!" Hobbs was shaken right out of his usual calm.

"And they also manufacture dynamite sticks for quarry blasting," said Lemaitre. "They use the same cardboard, the same paper, the same packing that's been used in the bits and pieces we've found. No doubt about it—look!"

He took a plastic bag out of his pocket. In this were some tattered scraps of paper, torn cardboard, and a piece of fuse. All of these were blackened and burned. He shook them out onto a sheet of paper on Gideon's desk, then drew out another plastic bag containing the same kind of thing in an unburned state.

"They're identical. I've had 'em up in the lab." He rubbed his hands together as he went on, "Enough to justify a search at the offices of The Simple Brethren, George? They don't call themselves that to the public. Marriott runs a Bible society—sells Bibles to underdeveloped countries for next to nothing, but old Chaplin says he holds meetings there. He has a flat in Victoria, too, opposite the R.C. cathedral. How about a search warrant for both places?"

"The quicker the better," Gideon agreed. "We want the offices closely watched, too."

"I've had 'em covered since yesterday morning," Lemaitre told him jubilantly. "Everyone who goes there is watched and followed, but don't worry, they don't know they're under surveillance."

That was the first time Gideon had any real misgivings about Lemaitre's overconfidence. Nothing would be served by saying so, he could only pray.

"We want to raid both places at the same time," he said. "Which one do you want, Lem?" He was already at the telephone, dialing Scott-Marle's office.

"The offices."

"Right. Alec, you take the other—hullo, sir. Gideon. I'd like search warrants sworn for two places in Victoria, the offices of . . ."

As he talked, Lemaitre and Hobbs went out together to make arrangements for the raids. There seemed to be a briskness in Hobbs's movements which hadn't been evident for weeks.

Scott-Marle said, "I'll see to these at once, Commander." To hear him, one would think that he was promising action on some matter of routine.

At his desk in the flat, Hector Marriott was reading some tracts which he himself had written when his telephone bell rang. He did not answer it immediately, but finished reading before slowly lifting the instrument.

"This is Hector Marriott."

"Brother Marriott," a man said, and Marriott recognized Joliffe's voice. "We are being watched and followed by the police. I have no doubt of it. There are watchers in the street

outside your flat now. Will you consider leaving at once?"
There was a breathlessness in the usually calm voice.

Marriott said calmly, "If you are right, yes."

"There is no doubt, Brother Marriott," Joliffe asserted. "Go
to the window and see for yourself. There are two men at a
manhole; they are police officers."

"Your word is enough for me," Marriott said calmly. "You
will also leave, making sure that the names and addresses of
the Brothers are not left intact."

"I will see to that."

"Then we will meet after our final acts of atonement,"
Marriott said.

When he replaced the receiver he stepped to the window
and looked out. Two men were at a manhole, exactly as
Joliffe had said. One of them was looking up at the flat, as if
casually. Marriott made no attempt to conceal himself, glancing up and down the street, then drawing back. He picked up
a black brief case, hooked an umbrella over his arm, and put
his bowler hat on, very straight. He went out, not toward the
lift but toward the stairs. He walked through a doorway
marked "Emergency Exit," crossed a landing where the stairs
led up and down, crossed to another door, and was now in a
different wing of the building. He walked along to the nearest
lift, and pressed the "up" button. In two minutes he was in
another flat which overlooked the street from a very different
angle. He took off his hat, hung it up with his umbrella, and
sat at a table on which there was only an inkstand and a writing pad.

Lemaitre stepped out of his car in Victoria Street and took
a quick look round. Several Yard and Divisional men were in
sight, everything was going as planned. With two inspectors,
a sergeant, and a detective officer, he went into the building
where The Simple Brethren had their office. A man in painter's overalls carrying a brush and paint pot said:

"Still up there, sir."

"Good." Lemaitre climbed the stairs two at a time, and
reached a door marked BIBLES FOR SIMPLE FOLK. He did not
waste a second in trying the handle, found the door locked,
beckoned another, heavier man, and whispered, "Let's get it
down. Try it with our shoulders first." They put their shoulders to the flimsy-looking door, drew back, and launched their
full weight.

The door gave way.

As they staggered in, a sheet of flame shot out from a steel
filing cabinet in a corner where a man was standing, working

furiously. In another room, two men were ripping paper across and across.

"Stop 'em!" Lemaitre roared. He rushed to the filing cabinet, pushed the man aside, pulled out the drawer in which papers were burning, and emptied it with quick deliberation on to the floor. Fire licked at his hands and face but he took no notice, methodically treading the flames out. Other policemen had come in, and the two men from the inner room were already handcuffed.

An inspector said, "I'll do that, sir."

Lemaitre nodded gratefully and rushed to the other room. Here papers had been taken out of drawers and piled up for burning; others had been torn to shreds. Lemaitre went to one filing cabinet which was untouched so far and began to go through it. Suddenly he sprang round, snatched up a telephone, and dialed the Yard.

"Gimme Commander Gideon!" He was almost exulting. "Hurry, hurry, hurry! . . . Hallo, George! . . . We've got their names and addresses and a marked list of churches—"

"And some dynamite sticks," a man whispered in his ear.

"And dynamite!" Lemaitre roared. "If Alec's got *his* man we're home and dry."

Hobbs, less ostentatious in every way, was just as decisive. He examined the lock of the door at Marriott's flat, a Yale which would take time they did not have to force. He stood aside and beckoned to men who held jimmies. They started on the door, levering at it vigorously, as Hobbs pressed the bell. He heard nothing except the crunching wood and the occasional sound of metal on metal. As the door swung open he was the first to step inside, and he moved very quickly. It took him less than thirty seconds to discover that the flat was empty.

Within an hour, arrests were being made all over London. From their homes, their offices, their shops, The Simple Brethren were taken by the police, and all premises were searched. In each there was a quantity of dynamite. In some were cards bearing the name of a church, apparently the next to be attacked. In three there were marked lists of churches, and the police set the three men who had these lists aside for special interrogation—men named Joliffe, Abbotsbury and Dennison.

Nowhere was there any mention of Marriott, or of the Committee of Three, nothing more leading than tracts and in-

structions declaring the purpose of The Simple Brethren—
worship without ritual and without dogma of any kind.

By mid-afternoon, Gideon's desk was piled high with
papers.

"If only *one* of them would talk," Lemaitre said helplessly.

Gideon was at his most forbidding. "And if only we hadn't
let Marriott get away."

"We can't expect everything," Lemaitre protested.

"We need this man because of what he might do," Gideon
said ponderously.

"Can't do more than we are doing." Lemaitre, secure in the
greatness of his triumph, was sitting on a corner of the desk.
"There's a general call out, every paper and every television
channel will carry his photograph. We can't be long finding
him."

Gideon, inwardly more disturbed than he allowed Lemaitre
to see, turned over some paper as a telephone bell rang. He
picked up the receiver.

"Gideon . . . Oh, yes . . . Yes, Brixton . . . Who? . . .
Yes, I don't see why not." He put down the receiver and said,
"Entwhistle's changed his tune up to a point. He's asked if he
can get in touch with his employers, to get them to fix legal
aid for him."

"Suits us if it suits him," Lemaitre agreed. "Can't be much
of a firm if they haven't already done something about it off
their own bat. Pity we can't hang all murdering baskets," he
added. "Well, I'll see what else I can do."

He went out.

Gideon made a note in the Entwhistle case file.

Geoffrey Entwhistle, quite sober and very frightened now,
told a middle-aged, obviously skeptical solicitor the simple
truth, as they sat in his remand cell at Brixton Jail. At that
very moment, Eric Greenwood was standing by Bessie
Smith's desk, saying that it looked as if the police had caught
the sacrilegious devils. In the hospital at Tottenham, Dalby
was standing over his daughter, who looked pale and drawn,
her eyes darkly shadowed.

"I understand, Sally, I understand, and everything will be
all right. We'll let your mother go on thinking that you've
been away for a holiday."

A policewoman sitting in a corner said quietly, "The important thing is that your daughter should remember everything
she can, Mr. Dalby. There are so many other girls we have
not yet traced."

"I am sure she will help in every way," Dalby said. He bent down and kissed his daughter's forehead.

At Scotland Yard, Rollo was trying to make Toni Bottelli talk, but Bottelli had sunk into a sullen silence. Golightly was looking through the photographs in the cellar at Tottenham, and all the papers found on the premises, but no trace of the other missing girls had yet been found.

Golightly began to go through the stock of the shop itself, while the old crone who looked after it protested sibilantly. He found a section under one counter filled with envelopes marked:

CIGARETTES DIRECT FROM
THE MANUFACTURERS
BEST VIRGINIAN AND TURKISH
TOBACCO ONLY USED

He opened one of these to see what literature was enclosed —and found some of the most obscene photographs he had ever come across. His cheeks became tinged with red.

"My God, what a swine," he muttered. He tossed them across to another man who was taking sample packets of branded as well as "privately manufactured" cigarettes; these were going for analysis to the Yard, and if any contained drugs there would be another charge against Bottelli.

"We might find something from the suppliers of the tobacco, or drugs if there are any," Golightly remarked. "Keep at it."

While all this was going on, bands of voluntary workers were clearing up the debris in the churches, newspapers had more photographs than they could hope to cope with, headlines screamed news of The Simple Brethren and the mass of arrests, and every newspaper seemed to heave a sigh of relief, as if the worst was over.

Gideon did not feel so sanguine. Lemaitre did, with ample excuse. Hobbs preferred not to commit himself.

That evening Hector Marriott sat studying photographs of St. Paul's Cathedral. At the same time he made frequent references to a detailed plan of the main body of the church, the transepts, the galleries, and, particularly, the Whispering Gallery. He concentrated more and more on the Whispering Gallery and the various parts of the church which could be seen from it, including the inner dome with the Thornhill cartoons, the High Altar, and the baldachin. After a while he marked a spot on the Gallery with an X. From there the choir stalls and the High Altar would be clearly visible.

Finished, he moved into an adjacent bedroom and, kneeling, he prayed silently for a few minutes before rising and opening a drawer. He took out what looked like a camera, removed the lenses, and examined them. They were not in fact lenses, but containers of a particular kind of firework—nor was it a camera, but a light type of pistol.

He fitted in two cartridges. They would be fired simultaneously and would explode on contact with any hard object. He put the "camera" down on a table and took a suit out of the wardrobe. It was very different from the suits he usually wore, being of greenish-red tweed, the jacket belted over bulky knickerbockers. There was also a Tyrolean hat with a feather tucked in the narrow band, and a pair of brown shoes with thick rubber soles.

He contemplated these sartorial aberrations with a satisfied eye before again sinking to his knees in an attitude of prayer. After a long, long silence, his voice rose in supplication:

"When shall it be, O Lord? Grant me the vision that I may do Thy will on the appointed day."

CHAPTER 24
THE WHISPERING GALLERY

On Sunday evening, with no further progress made, Gideon flew to Paris.

On Monday morning there was a message from Dean Howcroft; would Commander Gideon be good enough to attend an emergency meeting of the Council of Advisers? The message reached Hobbs, who had come in after an early-morning cremation service at Hampstead Crematorium. He rang for Lemaitre, who came in as promptly as he would have had Gideon been there.

"What's on?" he asked.

Hobbs said, "Dean Howcroft wants one of us at a Council of Advisers. Are you free to go?"

Lemaitre stared. "I'm *free* enough, but you're GeeGee's stand-in."

Hobbs said stiffly, "Do you want to go, or don't you?"

Lemaitre, still oversensitive, drew himself up and answered sharply, "Naturally I want to go. Any idea what they're after?"

"No," Hobbs said. "It's for three o'clock this afternoon."

"Right. I'll be there." Lemaitre went off, and Hobbs stared out the window, wondering whether it was wise to send Lemaitre to such a meeting. He was not thinking as clearly as he liked; in at least one way he had sent Lemaitre because he himself did not feel able to cope.

Helen's death hurt more, infinitely more, than he had expected; the anguish of his loss, the emptiness of wasted years, was almost greater than he could bear.

Lemaitre, very self-conscious and for once unable to cover nervousness with an air of boisterous bonhomie and cocksureness, entered the room where the Council of Advisers was already waiting. He recognized all of them. There was something almost forbidding about each as they sat together round the table. They made him welcome and yet he had the feeling that they were acutely disappointed at Gideon's absence.

At last the Chairman Bishop said, "Mr. Lemaitre, we have two decisions to make, and in one of them we shall be guided by your advice." He paused, to cough. "Simply this: there is a certain amount of evidence to suggest that the emergency is over, and that the police have made so many arrests that there is little more to fear. It has been suggested that we should not continue with our precautions; at the same time, we do not want to take any grave risk. What is your opinion?"

"Shouldn't think there's any risk for the smaller places," Lemaitre answered promptly. "Wouldn't like to say the same about the cathedrals and the Abbey while this chap Marriott is about. He's liable to try anything."

"But you think we can safely relax the vigilance at the smaller churches? It will be a great relief to many people who are freely giving time they can ill afford to spare."

"Relax it slowly," advised Lemaitre. "You can't be absolutely sure Marriott hasn't got a special hate. He was a member of the C. of E. once." He sat back, satisfied and pleased with himself, now quite at home. "What's the other problem?"

"That is one of a rather more delicate nature," the Bishop said. "We are, all of us, concerned for the men who have been arrested. We know they have committed grievous offenses, against the law and against the churches we represent, but nevertheless they are human beings. There are rumors of very undue pressure being brought to bear on them, so as to make them talk. . . ."

Lemaitre slapped his hand on the table, loudly enough to betray his anger.

"I soon told them where to get off," he reported to Hobbs, an hour later. "Undue pressure, with Gideon in control! I let 'em have it, I can tell you."

"They don't know Gideon as well as you do," Hobbs said dryly. "How about the cathedrals and the Abbey? Have you doubled our patrols on them?"

"Yep! Every place of vantage is covered, there's no need to worry about that."

"Good," said Hobbs, trying to force enthusiasm into his voice. "Now, why don't you go and get some sleep? You've been at it night and day too long."

"Like an echo of Gee-Gee, you are," remonstrated Lemaitre. "If it's okay by you, that's what I'll do."

He went off a few minutes later, and as soon as he had gone Hobbs pulled the telephone toward him and told the operator, "I will be out for the rest of the day. Don't try to find me. I'll call in from time to time."

"Yes, sir, but—"

"I'm in a hurry," Hobbs said irritably.

"There's a call from Paris coming through for you now, sir. From Mr. Gideon. Will you take it?"

Hobbs sat down heavily. "Yes. Put him through." Almost immediately there came a voice speaking in almost incomprehensible French, followed by Gideon, saying, "Are you there, Scotland Yard? Are you—"

"No one's blown us up yet," Hobbs said mildly.

"Who—oh, Alec. Alec," repeated Gideon, "I've been looking through one of the catalogues put out by Marriott's pyrotechnics firm. They make warning lights, miniature Very lights as well as fireworks, and some of them are very small. They've two or three varieties which expel a pellet which only catches fire on contact. That's the kind of thing Marriott might use if he can't get close enough to the place he wants to damage. So all points of vantage from galleries at any height want close watching."

"I'm going to have them checked personally," Hobbs said. In a few minutes, he was on his way.

He went first to Westminster Abbey, up into all the galleries, where plain-clothes men as well as churchmen were on duty twenty-four hours a day. He was accompanied by the

Dean himself, for once unmoved by the transcending beauty
of the church as he pointed out every likely place from which
great damage could be done. It seemed to Hobbs that the
greatest harm would be caused from the Muniment Room,
from which the High Altar and the Sanctuary could be seen,
and he stationed two more men there. He went to the Roman
Catholic Cathedral, doubled the police guard at the gallery
entrances, and was assured by the head sacristan that every
possible precaution was being taken. Satisfied, Hobbs drove to
St. Paul's.

It was crowded with tourists.

He went first to the higher galleries and then to the Whispering Gallery, the most obvious place from which to attack
the High Altar at a distance. The whole length seemed to be
alive with murmurings as of the waves of the sea. Hundreds
of people were there, young and old, English and European,
American and Asian, most of them apparently intent on the
wonder of the great dome and intrigued by the way in which
every sound reverberated. There was a German party at the
main entrance.

Hobbs went to the outdoor gallery where men stood on
duty, making sure no one could climb the columns supporting
the dome or approach from the roof of the nave. It was a
pleasant day. No one seemed to notice the plain-clothes men.
He went back into the gallery and walked about it, peering
through the intricate wrought-iron work, deciding that the
view immediately opposite the High Altar was likely to be the
danger spot. From here, so much of the Cathedral was vulner-
able.

Then he saw a weakness in their defense.

The plain-clothes men were always on the move, mixing
with tourists while paying particular attention to any man on
his own. Yet it would take Marriott only a second to point an
ejector such as Gideon had mentioned and aim from the gallery opposite the altar. If a man were so to aim he would un-
doubtedly want to be as central as he could, to make sure he
caused the greatest possible damage. Hobbs checked this position, doubled back, and went up to the Chief Inspector in
charge of the police on duty.

He said in an aloof way, "Why aren't you carrying out Mr.
Lemaitre's instructions accurately?"

The man was Detective Inspector Goodways of the
City Police, under the Yard's authority for this particular task. He was big, middle-aged, experienced, and well
trained, and he replied at once, "I thought we were, sir."

"Two men ought to be over there," Hobbs pointed to the

central vantage point. "Didn't Mr. Lemaitre give those precise instructions? I'm sure he did."

"Er—"

"All right, if you forgot you forgot," Hobbs said. "Make sure the men are there from now on. And watch out for any man who appears to be taking a photograph through the railings, or for anyone who puts his hands to his pocket—or inside his jacket—where he might keep something to throw."

"Very good, sir." Goodways showed no sign of his resentment.

Hobbs went off, knowing he had left the man fuming inwardly, but considering it worthwhile. It might be hard on this man, but it would do him no harm; whereas if anything were to go wrong because of a glaring oversight by Lemaitre, it would have grave repercussions on Gideon's chief assistant and Lemaitre would never forgive himself. Hobbs already glimpsed something of the way Gideon got the best out of his men, and he had a feeling that Gideon would approve of what he had done today.

Hobbs left the Cathedral, still worried, but unable to see anything more he could do.

As he went down the steps opposite the Great West Door, a touring party of Germans or Austrians came up. One of them moved from one side to join the main group, but Hobbs saw nothing strange in that and flagged down a taxi.

Hector Marriott went in with the crowd of tourists.

Marriott waited until the group was dispersing after being shown the American Roll of Honor and the Tijou Sanctuary Screens, then made his way toward the entrance to the winding staircase leading to the Whispering Gallery. He looked about him all the time, knowing that many of the people nearby were police and cathedral guards, fully aware that he would have only a second or two in which to carry out his mission. He did not hurry even when he reached the gallery but went round to the section above the choir, bent down to look through the railings, pointed his camera, and pretended to take pictures. Then he strolled round toward the spot where Hobbs had stationed the two men. Nearby was Detective Inspector Goodways, still smarting, still not sure whether he had indeed misunderstood Lemaitre—or whether Lemaitre had forgotten to tell him.

He watched the solitary tourist who had both hands on the camera with the very long lens attachments. He noticed, with his extra sensitiveness acquired in the past fifteen minutes, that this man seemed to be particularly intent. It was unusual for a German or an Austrian to break away from a group. Alerted, Goodways stepped forward as the man reached a spot exactly opposite the High Altar. The two detectives stationed at the rail moved forward too. None of them really suspected this man; they were simply taking precautions.

He bent down.

"Excuse me, sir," Detective Inspector Goodways said.

As he spoke, he saw the other's body tense, saw that instead of straightening up, as would normally have been the case, he bent lower, thrusting the lens with determined calculation through the wrought iron. On that instant Goodways realized the awful truth. He let out a great bellow and leapt forward. At the same moment an eerie booming filled the gallery and the great dome, echoing and echoing to the clamor of the oncoming police. Goodways grabbed the strap of the "camera," jolting the man backward, saw the lens pointing to the roof, and waited breathlessly for the roar he feared would come.

The "camera" dropped from Marriott's hands. He twisted round, glaring at his assailant. Goodways pulled again at the strap but Marriott suddenly ducked, put his head through the loop, and raced for the exit. He thrust one policeman aside, dodging and turning from others blocking his path. People were shouting, children screaming, there was pandemonium in the gallery and down in the great nave.

Marriott saw one chance: the outer gallery. He ran toward it with police pounding after him. He got through. Beyond was the mighty panorama of London, the shimmering Thames, the great new buildings, the countless spires; in the distance, far beyond the great bridges of Blackfriars, Waterloo and Hungerford, were the outlines of Big Ben, the Houses of Parliament, and the Abbey.

Footsteps thudded behind him.

Without a moment's hesitation he climbed onto the stone balustrade, poised, and dived downward.

CHAPTER 25
GIDEON'S HOPE

Gideon stepped off the plane at London Airport on Wednesday evening, was given all assistance in a perfunctory passage through Customs, and saw Lemaitre among the crowd at the rail beyond the Customs bay. Lemaitre, looking thoroughly pleased with himself, pumped Gideon's arm and led him away.

"How are the ladies of Paris these days? . . . Okay, don't tell me, don't tell me . . . Had a good trip? . . . Things have gone just right here, George. Had a bit of trouble with the hashish, Golightly's onto something there . . . Found where those girls go to, too . . . Yes, fact. They get drugs in tobacco from a little spot in the Middle East, can't say where in public or it would start a war . . . Excuse me, madam . . . In return, our white-slave hero, Bottelli, shipped girls over for the enjoyment and edification of European gentlemen who can't get all they want in Europe . . . Fact, George. They sign an agreement and go over as chorus girls. Yes, we've talked to some of them . . . First of all Bottelli made a selection, then after doping the kids he took his pictures, after which he did his deal with them . . . Eh?"

They were getting into his car. Gideon said, "What about the Dalby girl?"

"She's okay now. Needs time to recover but the medicos say she won't remember much."

"The three dead girls?"

"They threatened to talk, so he gave 'em an overdose of Veronal—young Rhodes got the drug for him."

"Does Bottelli admit that?"

"Yes. Rollo worked a miracle on him."

Gideon grunted as he sat back in the car. "Anything else?"

"Entwhistle was committed for trial this morning, at the Old Bailey. He did it all right."

"Looks like it," Gideon said slowly, conscious of a stirring within him, faint but persistent.

"The hashish and the tobacco have been coming in by air, so I've just been talking to the Airport Police and Customs . . . No problem. The church trouble's a thing of the past," Lemaitre rattled on airily. "And we're the white-haired boys of the ecclesiastical pundits. Makes a nice change!"

Gideon said, "Did Marriott say anything?"

"Didn't have time. He broke his neck."

Gideon said gravely, "You did a very neat job, Lem."

"Not so bad, was I?" said Lemaitre, not attempting to assume humility. "I'll tell you one thing, George."

"What?"

"Alec Hobbs isn't such a bad old basket."

Gideon glanced round quickly. "Getting on all right?"

"Better than I expected. Everyone seems to like him after

all. Doesn't throw his weight about as much as we expected he would, and he's on the ball, believe me, he's on the ball. Know what I think, George?"

"Go on."

"In a funny way, his wife's death helped. Everyone felt sorry about it and if you ask me, it's made him a bit more human."

"I dare say you're right," said Gideon slowly. "Anything new come along?"

"Nothing to worry about," said Lemaitre. "The Old Man wants to see you at ten o'clock in the morning, I can tell you that."

Sir Reginald Scott-Marle was at his desk when Gideon went to the office next morning. He stood up at once to shake hands, then motioned to a chair.

"How did the gold affair go, George?"

"As far as I can judge it's a storm in a teacup," Gideon reported. "Nothing that each country can't handle for itself with a bit of help from Interpol. Most of the others seemed to agree by the time the conference was over."

"Oh," said Scott-Marle. "Pity you went, then."

"Not a bit," said Gideon. "It cleared the air—and it enabled Hobbs and Lemaitre to get to know each other better."

"That's most encouraging," said Scott-Marle. "I'm very glad."

Gideon went down to his own office and found the usual pile of reports on his desk, including a request for him to telephone his opposite number in the City of London Police. He put a call in at once.

"Hallo, George," the other man said. "Bring any Paris lovelies back with you? . . . Sly old devil . . . I wanted a word about one of our chaps, Detective Inspector Goodways, the man who stopped Marriott shooting in St. Paul's."

"What about him?" asked Gideon.

"I'd like to recommend him for the George Medal, he took a hell of a risk. But he seems to think you chaps at the Yard have a down on him . . . Eh? . . . Well, apparently Hobbs tore a strip off him because he'd forgotten something Lemaitre *didn't* tell him to do . . . Yes, I said didn't . . ."

The City man explained in some detail, and in the course of the recital the obvious truth dawned on Gideon: that Hobbs had chosen this way to cover up the one essential thing which Lemaitre had overlooked. He was smiling broadly by the time the City man had finished.

Then: "Put through the commendation. We'll gladly support it."

"Splendid!" the City man enthused. "I didn't think you would disappoint our Dean."

Gideon said, puzzled: "Dean? What Dean?"

"Howcroft," said the other. "He seems to have formed a high opinion of you; and he's very pro-Goodways. By the way, he's coming to see you this afternoon."

"Goodways?"

"No. Dean Howcroft."

"Oh," said Gideon.

Howcroft arrived, by appointment, in the middle of the afternoon. His white hair was silkier and more pure-looking than ever, and his face had acquired, or resumed, a kind of gentleness, as of peace after storm. He sat down opposite Gideon, studied him closely, and then said, "Commander, the Council of Advisers would be most grateful for more advice from you."

"Anything I can do," said Gideon, warily.

"We are quite sure of that," said Howcroft. "We have all the warmest appreciation of your attitude and your good counsel. It is simply this. Since Marriott died as he did—I cannot help feeling that it was a merciful deliverance, for his trial would have been a most distressing *cause célèbre*—the members of his sect are, for the most part, without funds. We have discovered that most of them served God in their own way, however dreadfully mistaken that way was, and lived on a very modest stipend—paid by Marriott."

Gideon said, "I gathered he was rich."

"He was indeed. However, he left nothing to them in a will, having died intestate. At a very lengthy session this morning, all members of the Council of Advisers felt that we should contribute toward the cost of their defense. They were shamefully misguided, but—" He broke off and shrugged his shoulders. "Do you have any opinion about this proposal?"

Gideon sat back in his chair, contemplating the old man intently before he said, "Yes, Dean Howcroft, I have. I think it's very warming indeed. I only hope the day will come when all people of all religions will feel the way you and the Council do now. Then the world will really be a place to live in."

The old man's smile was both gentle and serene. "And you would be out of a job! But I felt sure you would feel like that," the Dean went on. "What a remarkably understanding man you are."

Gideon shuffled uncomfortably, as he was apt to do in the high moments of his life.

Late that evening he tried to find the words to tell Kate what Howcroft had said; she was the only person in the world whom he could possibly tell. The words wouldn't come—but Penelope did, bright-eyed and excited. There was to be a special mid-term examination for the near-misses, and she was to sit for it. She was sure she would pass this time.

Soon, Gideon's home resounded to the joyousness of her playing.

OTHER NOVELS BY

EDGAR AWARD
WINNER

J. J. Marric

			U.S.	CAN.
8197-4	**GIDEON'S DAY** J. J. Marric		2.95	3.50
8207-5	**GIDEON'S MONTH** J. J. Marric		2.95	3.50
8198-2	**GIDEON'S NIGHT** J. J. Marric		2.95	3.50
8226-1	**GIDEON'S RISK** J. J. Marric		2.95	3.50
8199-0	**GIDEON'S WEEK** J. J. Marric		2.95	3.50
8234-2	**GIDEON'S MARCH** J. J. Marric		2.95	3.50
8247-4	**GIDEON'S VOTE** J. J. Marric		2.95	3.50
8258-X	**GIDEON'S LOT** J. J. Marric		2.95	3.50

Buy them at your local bookstore or use this convenient coupon for ordering:

STEIN AND DAY/ *Publishers*
Briarcliff Manor, NY 10510
Sales Department

Please send me the books I have checked above. I am enclosing $ _____.
(Please add $1.00 per order to cover postage and handling.) Send check or money order— *no*
cash or C.O.D.s. Prices and numbers are subject to change without notice.

Name _____
Address _____
City _____ State _____ Zip _____

Allow 6 weeks for delivery.